Deadl

Also by Gaelyn Gordon

For adults
Above Suspicion
Strained Relations
Last Summer
Fortune's Fool

For teenagers
Stonelight
Prudence M Muggeridge, Damp Rat
Mindfire
Tripswitch
The Other Worlds of Andrew Griffin
River Song

For children
Tales from Another Now
Several Things are Alive and Well and Living in Alfred Brown's Head
Take Me to Your Leaders
Magginty
Fuss Finds Out (illus. Clare Bowes)
Fuss the Farm Dog (illus. Clare Bowes)
David and the Monster from Outer Space (illus. Clare Bowes)
Walter and the Too Big Dog (illus. Clare Bowes)
Robert's Robot (illus. John Tarlton)
Fuss the Collector (illus. Clare Bowes)
Fuss and Friend (illus. Clare Bowes)

Picture books
Duckat (illus. Chris Gaskin)
Fortunate Flats (illus. John Tarlton)

Deadlines

Gaelyn Gordon

DL

Apart from involuntary exposure to news media, the author's only knowledge of the workings of the police force has been gleaned from fiction. Any resemblance, therefore, between the police as depicted in this novel and those in real life is purely coincidental... It would also be rather alarming.

On the other hand, the author has some first-hand knowledge of both the world of writers and academia, and is on a firmer footing in assuring the reader that no resemblance is intended between any character in this book and any character who actually exists.

David Ling Publishing Limited
PO Box 34-601
Birkenhead, Auckland 10

The publisher gratefully acknowledges the assistance of Creative New Zealand.

First Edition
Deadlines

ISBN 0-908990-32-4

First published 1996

Typeset by ExPress Communications Limited
Printed in New Zealand

For Carol

one

In his modestly luxurious hideaway in the hills above Melbourne, Frederick Tapper, that phenomenon of modern literature whose works were not only studied in universities all round the English-speaking world but also enjoyed by hundreds of thousands of avid – ordinary – readers, switched on his computer and sat staring at the blank screen.

His hands clenched in his lap. How did he used to start? What had happened to all those wicked ideas about other characters, situations that had boiled and bubbled through his thoughts while he was working on something else? His mind had positively seethed with possibilities. He'd caught them as they'd gone by, jotted them down into the IDEAS file to get them out of the way of what he was currently writing. But now – he sighed and called up IDEAS, skimmed through it yet again. As usual, nothing that was there grabbed him – he couldn't even remember what he'd intended when he wrote some things. *There's this woman who works making fish fingers.* Now what the hell had he meant by that?

How could he have been so complacent, so certain that he'd understand his cryptic notes? God, he'd just thrown them into the file and left them there to rot – he'd never seriously considered that he'd need to use them; there was always something fresh, something demanding attention...

Work, he told himself. *Get to it. Anything.* His hands hovered over the keys. 'FISH-FINGER FACTORY' they typed. Shit! He deleted the words and went to make himself another cup of coffee.

He was still drinking it when his housekeeper arrived, and with her his mail. Well, that was something.

Yet another letter from Julia, his agent. Julia the ever-hopeful. How were things going? Long time no hear. She'd nearly phoned last week,

7

Freddie was that much on her mind. Was there something wrong? The new novel? Would Freddie like her to fly over? There'd be the film contract to sign in a week or so and Julia could bring that with her rather than mail it; of course Julia realised that there was nothing that couldn't be done by fax, but she did have a couple of clients in Oz who could do with a visit and she'd really love to see Freddie again.

Frederick sniffed. Julia's company was the last thing he wanted at this stage, lolloping around the house, wagging her tail whenever she caught Frederick's eye, panting with anxiety whenever Frederick was not at the computer. Frederick had a mental flash of Julia curled up at his feet while he worked, scrabbling and whining to be let into his bedroom at nights.

He scrawled off a note – *Fax film contract. I'll check it; you can sign. Too busy for visit. Working. Warmest, F.T.*, and fed it into the fax.

The rest of the mail was the usual – but it included an ominously bulky package from New Zealand. The customs declaration read *manuscript, value NIL*.

Yet another hopeful, just wanting advice. Just wanting to take a day or two out of a busy man's life to read the humble offering, and expecting him to waste another few hours writing screeds of admiring instruction. They should be so bloody lucky. He undid the seal carefully – if there was no return postage he could reseal it and post it NO LONGER AT THIS ADDRESS, RETURN TO SENDER.

Included with the typescript was a padded addressed envelope and international reply coupons. That was something. But they didn't consider, did they, that Frederick would have to go to a post office to cash the coupons in for stamps?

He took a business card from the kitchen desk, wrote, *Sorry, no time to read this, F.T.* and clipped it to the title page. *THE PUNGENT COLLECTION a novel by Joseph Bradley.* Good title.

Idly – anything rather than face that empty grey screen – Frederick flicked over to the start of Chapter One. The first paragraph had him hooked. He read to the end of the chapter, standing there in the kitchen moving aside from time to time as the housekeeper bustled around him. At the close of the chapter, he took the manuscript with him into his office.

The covering note apologised for taking Mr Tapper's time, but Joseph Bradley was at a loss as to how to proceed. He had written novels before and had not done anything with them. They were rather in the nature of a hobby, just to fill in time during long vacations (Joseph Bradley earned his bread and butter at a university and was not one of those who sought feverishly after promotion by plunging into recondite and useless research). He had never shown his work to others, and even this novel had not been read by anyone else.

But this time I feel my work may be worthy of a readership. The novel is, I feel, nearly "getting there".

I have been a long-time admirer of Frederick Tapper's work, and, as will be obvious as you read, have been very influenced by it. This is why I am taking the liberty of sending you the manuscript. I feel that you may be able to advise me whether it is worth my while continuing to write.

Frederick settled back into his chair and read on.

The housekeeper brought his lunch in; he ate, hardly noticing. It was mid-afternoon before he finished. It wasn't just "nearly getting there"; this novel had arrived. It was brilliant – smooth, deceptively easy, wickedly ironic, subtle. He could have written it himself.

He wished he had.

Well, Joseph Bradley had kept him entertained for a whole working day; Frederick had better tell the bastard he was a writer. He switched his computer on again and started a letter.

Congratulations. "The Pungent Collection" is a delight. I found the ease of your writing...

Bloody hell. Bloody hell and shit and damn the bloody bastard. The ease of his writing – who the hell said it was easy? Tossed it off in his holidays, did he? Thought he was going to carry on where Frederick Tapper left off? Frederick Tapper was buggered if he was going to leave off; he was going through a perfectly normal dry patch, that was all.

Frederick's throat tightened with misery. It wasn't fair. This book – if only *he'd* thought of it. Thought of it first. Now this – he glanced at the covering letter again – this mealy-mouthed, prissy, second-rate lecturer was... Roast him. Boil the bugger and his clever ideas in – in smoking mutton fat.

No. No, don't do that. Just... Frederick's heart skipped a beat or two. Why not? He deleted what he'd so far written and started again.

Thank you for sending me the manuscript of "The Pungent Collection". I have read it, and consider it not without promise – though you have still some distance to travel before your work is publishable.

I hope that does not sound too disheartening – it's not intended to be so. I am not saying that you are no writer – I am convinced by what I have read that you will one day produce very readable work if you continue "plugging away." Writing is, as you'll have realised by now, a craft that you learn as you go along.

I am genuinely pleased that you thought of sending it to me because it comes at a time when I have decided to share some of the things that I have learnt "on the job" with aspiring writers who show a degree of competence, and I have a proposal to put to you along these lines...

I would like to suggest that you send me copies of the earlier novels you mention, dating each one so that I can see how your work has progressed. This will help me make an fuller assessment of where your skills lie and where I could perhaps be of help.

Was that too blatant? Would Joseph Bradley be suspicious of why an eminent author should take trouble over a non-entity? Frederick re-read the guy's letter. There was a certain smugness; would his feeling of superiority be enough for him not to question the offer? He wasn't a fool – a fool couldn't have written this novel; on the other hand some very clever writers had amazing blind spots when it came to real life...

One last thing. Might I suggest that you continue to keep your ambitions, and your writing, secret at this stage? Publishing is a notoriously fickle business, and even if you do improve, there is no guarantee that your novels will see the light of day. I say this only to save you possible embarrassment in the future. And I'm sure you'll appreciate why I do not wish the fact that I'm "taking apprentices" to be made public. The thought of great wads of unsolicited and inexpert manuscripts arriving on my doorstep is most unpleasant.

*Thank you for the courtesy of including return postage. I will,
however, keep the ms for the time being so that I can compare
it with your earlier work if my proposal meets with your
approval.*

He wondered, as the printer hummed, just what he thought he was
playing at. Delaying tactics, of course. Anything to keep the sod from
submitting that book to a publisher – who'd jump at it. But he couldn't
go on delaying for ever... Hell, he wouldn't need to – just until the
empty space where whatever-it-was lurked filled up with ideas again.

No question of plagiarising, however tempting it might be. Still,
if he had the whole of Joseph Bradley's work... and if Joseph Bradley
were to drop dead... Some hope! Frederick went to mix himself a
Pernod. He took it onto the balcony to sit in the sun for a quiet think.

two

"...of considerable influence in the latter half of the seventeenth century." Another lecture over. Joseph Bradley picked up the pages, placed them in their folder and started toward the lecture room door which was already jammed with students hustling their way out. Common courtesy was something Joseph had long ceased to expect from the dirty rabble he faced every day.

Not, he thought, as he entered the senior common room, that the students were much less uncouth than his colleagues. He noted the hush that greeted his entrance. They'd been talking about him – the whole lot of them, not just the English staff. Well, he was not going to give them the satisfaction of freezing him away from facilities he had every right to use. Since he'd arrived here, he had met with nothing but hostility from the staff. Condescension. "Friendly" enquiries about his research, when he'd already made it perfectly clear that *he* was not intending to waste his time preparing papers for second-rate academic publications. Then there had been the offers to come and have dinner with the wife and kids – when everyone was perfectly aware that Joseph was without (*thankfully* without) any such encumbrances.

"Bring your coffee over here, Joe." McCarthy, big, jolly, boorish, sitting with the O'Toole bitch and the new Junior Lecturer whose specialty was New Zealand literature. (*He'd* be teaching the works of Joseph Bradley before he was much older, and how would he like that?) McCarthy was far enough away for Joseph to affect, convincingly, not to have heard. *Joe.* For two pins, he'd point out that his name was Joseph, but that would entail tedious conversation. He chose a copy of *Punch* from the rack and sat with his back to the window.

Over the top of the magazine, he watched his colleagues. McCarthy's daughter, a leggy girl in school uniform, came in to look for her father.

McCarthy was obviously introducing her proudly to the new Fellow. He pulled her down to sit beside him on the sofa, put his arm round her shoulders and said something that made her giggle. The two of them, putting on a show of family affection for the benefit of onlookers, it made Joseph sick. On the other hand...

He finished his coffee and went out to his car. This time he drove round to his house, cruising slowly past to check that all seemed well. The lawns needed mowing, he'd get the agent to call them about that. And – he braked to make sure – there was a child's tricycle on the porch! He had particularly stipulated no children. He had packed his more fragile treasures away in the small bedroom, but the finely polished floors – the thought of children running, driving pedal cars perhaps, scarring the varnish, spilling food – paints! – on Joseph's rugs... His head was tight with anger. He swung the car away, checked in the rear vision mirror, and drove straight to the estate agents.

They phoned the tenants immediately. Yes, there was a child there at the moment, but he had come with his mother who was visiting for the afternoon. Of course the lawns weren't mown – it had been raining for some days.

"The lease agreement was perfectly clear," said Joseph. "No children. No children whatsoever. And the upkeep was to be meticulous."

Well, the estate agent would ring them later – it would be rather embarrassing for them with the mother of the child actually in the house if he were to phone again right now. But children of visitors – well, that was rather a grey area in the agreement, wasn't it? You couldn't expect...

But Joseph *did* expect. *No* children, and *no* pets. "If a dog were to defecate on a Persian rug, urinate on a Victorian cabinet, I presume you would consider it permissible if it were merely a visiting dog?" And, while he was there, Joseph would like to mention the flat he was currently renting. There was insufficient covering over the gutter in the street.

Ah, yes. The tenant of the flat that adjoined Mr Bradley's had already left a message about that. The agent intended to get in touch with the landlord and see what could be done.

Joseph hoped that something *would* be done – and done sharpish. As he left the office he distinctly heard the agent say, "Mr Bloody Up-yourself."

He did not demean himself by turning back to let the wretch know his *voce* had not been sufficiently *sotto*. So he did not notice the estate agent shift the request for a culvert from the Urgent to the Get Round To It Someday pile.

Once back in his flat, Joseph went straight to his word-processor. This evening he would indulge himself for an hour or so, writing a long letter to Frederick Tapper. Not that he would send it straight away; he would wait, naturally, to hear the great man's reaction to his manuscript, which would surely arrive any day now. Joseph would write mostly about Frederick's work, leaving his own efforts modestly aside. It would be well for Frederick to see how sensitively Joseph responded to his writing, how perceptive he was.

But first... Joseph called up a file that he had protected with a series of passwords and typed a brief note.

I feel it is important to point out to you that your husband's interest in his teenage daughter is unwholesome. You may not be aware that he is meeting her at various venues outside the family home.

He opened a drawer, took out and put on a pair of gloves, slid a sheet of A4 from the centre of the pile where there was no danger of his fingers' having touched it, and ran off a copy. Then he looked up the university address list and typed an envelope to Mrs Waldorf McCarthy.

He saved the note on file. Dangerous, he knew, but he enjoyed looking over what he had written from time to time almost as much as he enjoyed his letters' impact on their recipients. McCarthy's jollity would be considerably subdued in a day or two. He might even, as Jones and the pusillanimous Hancock had done, find himself facing divorce proceedings. Or worse... incest was such a popular crime these days.

Jones and Hancock. They had been skulking together in the common room recently. Had they been comparing notes? (Joseph Bradley smiled wryly at his unintentional pun.) Jones had been quite a close friend of that perverted junior lecturer, Hale, who'd done away with himself shortly after the Council had received a letter suggesting his grading practices could do with investigation. Would Jones and Hancock have thought of Joseph? Would they have gone to the police? It was the possibility of this sort of thing's happening that had prompted Joseph's move to the poky flat with the attendant indignities of having to deal with estate agents.

"Mr Bloody Up-yourself," indeed. Joseph typed another note:

Barton and Banks, estate agents, of Marlin Street, are regularly concealing around 20% of the revenue they receive as commission on sales.

He typed an envelope to the Department of Inland Revenue, put stamps on both letters – always an awkward task when one was forced to use gloves – and put them beside his computer to post later in the evening after he had written his letter to Frederick Tapper.

Detective Senior Sergeant Rangi Robert's blue Jap import (small but smart) turned into the driveway of the flats, missing, as it had most days this week, one of the two narrow steel strips that straddled the gutter. There was a graunch of metal and a splash as the muffler dipped down the steep asphalt on the road side. Then a clang as it hit and mounted the concrete edging of the kerb. Detective Senior Sergeant Rangi Roberts swore. The car gathered speed and shot down the drive into the carport where it settled into place beside the vintage Jaguar whose owner, Rangi's new neighbour, regularly set the culvert strips further apart to accommodate his car's wider wheelbase. It was too wet for Rangi to be bothered going out to reset the covers now. He just hoped the weather had cleared by morning and he didn't bloody forget.

Rangi switched off the ignition and opened the door hard. It slammed into the maroon paint of the Jag. "Bastard," said Rangi. He hauled himself out and checked his door for damage. It seemed okay, but was there a scrape of blue on the side of the Jag? Rangi rubbed at it guiltily, but it didn't come off. He shrugged and went round to get the grocery bags out of the boot.

No umbrella of course – the morning had been blue and gold, the weather report optimistic. You couldn't rely on the met reports the way you'd been able to before they'd had to start making money. Rangi reckoned that they saved up the accurate forecasts and only let them out to people who were prepared to pay.

He collected three bags in each hand, closed the boot with his elbow, edged round the two overflowing rubbish bins at the side of the carport, hunched his shoulders and ran across squelching grass to the front door of his flat. The guttering was still blocked. A curtain of plump droplets rattled down between Rangi and the door. He moved through it and dumped the groceries beside the wall. As he bent to do so, he felt the instant chill of the heavy drops spattering through the seat of his pants. The keys were entangled in the thin plastic handle of one of the bags; he wrenched them free and stood up, water trickling past his collar and down his neck.

He opened the door, picked up the plastic bags and stood dripping in the narrow passageway, wondering what was different.

...It was tidy – that was what. Mum had been threatening to come round with Sonia or Marama and "give the place a good going over because you just don't get the time, Boy, with that job of yours."

Bugger. Rangi tried to remember if there was anything Mum shouldn't have seen lying around the flat. Well, if there was, he'd hear about it soon enough.

He went through to the kitchen, dumped the bags on the gleaming bench. A single rose, its stem thrust into a tiny vase, glowed on the pristine surface of the kitchen table. Underneath it a piece of paper smiled, "Kia ora, e tama." Rangi sighed. It had been a shit-awful day, and now this.

He tried to push the day out of his mind as he stowed the groceries – hash browns, chicken thighs and a couple of tv dinners into the freezer compartment. Then he got the milk, butter and beer into the fridge. The fridge had been cleared out and smelt different. He squatted down to peer inside. A green plastic apple with a wick nestled against the vegetable box. "Fresh For Weeks" said its label. Rangi straightened up and sighed. There was a strange tin on top of the fridge. Rangi opened it. Great – cheese busters, Mum's specialty. The rest of the groceries could wait – he was going to have himself a cheese buster and a beer or two to wash the day away before he dealt with anything more.

The phone rang. Mum. Yeah, yeah, it had been a great surprise... yeah he was really grateful, and especially for the bikkies, eh. It was terrific to come home and... yeah, he'd seen the rose – real – yeah, well, he'd only just this minute got in and he was on the point of phoning her when... yeah? Jeez, not just Sonia and Marama but the Kaipara girls as well?... Yeah, it was really kind of them all... Yeah?... The whole day? He didn't reckon the flat'd been bad enough for five of them for a whole day...

He shouldn't have said that. Mum took a long time telling him why it had taken so long. Rangi's eyes swivelled from the kitchen, where his beer was waiting, to the ceiling. Cobweb in the corner – they'd missed that, hadn't they?

Yeah, Mum... yeah really great. Cool... As much rubbish as that, eh? Well, it did sort of pile up when you were busy... so... in the spare bin? There wasn't a spare bin, Mum... That one? But that belonged to the guy in the other flat, he seemed to like to keep it Rangi's side of the carport... no, of course Mum had done the right thing... no Rangi didn't expect her to drive through town with bags of his rubbish spilling out the car... yeah, well, the guy's bin *would* be empty, wouldn't it; it was only yesterday the rubbish was collected... Yeah, Rangi's bin was still full because he hadn't had time to put it out yesterday – pressure of work, eh... no, not to worry, he'd see the guy... sure he'd understand... he probably had hardly any rubbish anyway... No, Rangi was not telling Mum she was an interfering old...

A packet of what?... Yeah, well, he used them... you had to eh, unless you *wanted* to get a girl... yeah, well, maybe they shouldn't've been out there in the open like that, but Rangi didn't know Mum was going to bring the girls... yeah, well, so if it was Mum found them then there was no harm done eh... "Christ, Mum!"... Yeah, sorry about the language, but –

Look, there was someone at the back door... he'd have to... yeah, he was just that grateful... it'd been a terrific surprise... of course he'd do his best to keep it like that now that... Yeah, well, look they were knocking real hard, he'd have to go... Yeah, not the weekend, though – he was on duty. Off tomorrow, but he had things that he had to... Yeah, he would get round soon – he'd ring her. And love to Dad, eh. And thank the girls, won't you?

It was the neighbour at the door, the Jag owner. About the rubbish bin. Bald head, glasses over popping blue eyes, pretty little mouth under a most unfortunate nose. Some sort of shaving rash or something that ran up the neck and cheeks. Rangi decided not to ask him in for a beer. "I just heard about it," he said. "It was my Mum, see. She –"

"One doesn't like to complain; one always makes an effort to preserve good relationships with one's neighbours." The mouth flicked upwards into a brief condescending smile. "But good relationships are based on a common acceptance of ground rules. And it is a fairly obvious ground rule that where people live in close proximity there must be a scrupulous observation of the rights of property." What was this guy? Nobody *spoke* like that. As though aware of Rangi's thought, the neighbour simplified his message, speaking slowly and carefully. "*My* rubbish bin, for example, is not *your* rubbish bin, though they may 'rub shoulders' in the carport. You may be used to common property where you come from, but it's different in the town." The mouth closed primly.

Where you come from. Rangi hadn't heard that sort of thing in years. Did the guy realise what he'd said? Rangi heard blood singing in his ears. He took a deep breath and then remembered the fleck of blue on polished maroon paintwork. "Look," he said. "I'm going up to the supermarket now. I'll get you another bin, okay?"

That wasn't the point, though it was the least Rangi could do. And about shifting the metal plates at the entrance to the drive. While he was here, the neighbour wanted to mention a thing or two about that. The Jaguar was old, valuable and low slung. Would Rangi kindly leave the plates where they were. Correctly spaced for the car's wheel base.

"Reckon it's the landlord's problem." said Rangi. "We need a bigger one, eh? Long one, not two titchy little things like that. I've already phoned the agents about it. And the guttering."

"Guttering?"

"Blocked – rain spilling over right by the front door. Regular torrent."

There was nothing wrong with the neighbour's guttering. He'd cleared out his side last week when he'd moved in. It shouldn't be too much for a fit young type like Rangi to nip up a ladder and clean it out. He would find the obstruction easy to clear as it would consist only of leaves. Autumn might be mists and mellow fruitfulness in the country, but in the town it was merely wretched weather and leaves in the guttering. One didn't surely expect the estate agents who had the leasing of the property to come running round to carry out little jobs like that. Still, he agreed with Rangi that there should be a more appropriate metal culvert. And the neighbour looked forward to receiving a new rubbish bin. "You're on your way to get it now, are you?"

The bloody things cost nearly forty bucks.

On the way back, Rangi was so careful not to miss the right hand culvert that the passenger side clanged into the gutter.

He dropped off the bin, which was received with a complacent nod. "I'm working at the moment," the neighbour said importantly. Rangi went back to his flat and left yet another message about culverts on the estate agent's answer phone, then shoved a tv dinner into the oven and started on the beer and busters.

His shoulders were damp. Summer was over. On the second can he let his mind slide back into the day. Sir was not pleased. Rangi had shown promise – great promise. Two murders solved almost single-handed, with only a few hints from Sir how to go about them. But since then, what? Bugger all, that's what. Rangi was missing the obvious every time. Dead wood was what he was turning out to be. Okay at routine hack work, but it was others who were putting two and two together. And he had to realise that his rapid promotion – deserved at the time, of course – made him a target for others' complaints, and complaints there had been...

Rangi wriggled his shoulders. He'd been lucky with the two cases – just lucky that was all. Things just sort of dropped into his lap. *He'd* never asked for promotion – just got it. That'd been luck, too, he reckoned – though he hadn't done too badly at the exams. And Sir was always on about "sheer plod." The routine stuff being the essence of police work. And he was okay at routine – Sir said so himself.

The oven buzzed and Rangi turned on the television. He'd watch the game show while he ate, get himself out of worrying.

The show was unsettling. All those toothy grins, all that hype. People enjoying themselves. He looked for the morning's newspaper to see what was on at the movies, but it had been tidied permanently out of sight. In the bin, probably. In any case, there was nobody to go with; Rangi was between women at the moment. He sighed. That was another thing wrong with life.

At least they hadn't tossed out the tv guide – he found it stowed on the magazine rack of the coffee table. There was bugger all on.

Too early for bed.

Maybe he could ring some of his mates, see if any of them felt like a hand or two of cards. But at the moment they were all well set up with company of their own – married most of them.

Maybe he could cruise down town, see if there was any action.

He sat staring at a family comedy show for a while and then realised that the only thing he was taking in was the ads. Shit. He got up, leaving the metal tray of the tv dinner on the floor beside his chair, and went to get his parka. Then he came back and picked up the tray, tossing the knife and fork in the sink as he dumped the tray in the kitchen tidy. There you are, Mum.

Pubs were open, but they were no fun if you didn't have company to start with. Besides, in his job, going into a pub to look for company was a no go. He cruised past the movie houses. Nothing on he wanted to see. The only other places open were the spacies parlours and the library.

Well, why not? He had a library card in his wallet from when he was still at school. He guessed they hadn't changed cards since then. Go to bed with a good book. Nothing else to go to bed with.

The library had been done up since he was last there. It was noisier now, too. People chatting away, no more sit down and shut up signs. Colourful. Brighter. There were kids playing with construction blocks and wooden toys. A gang of teenagers gossiped over magazines; some looked as though they were doing homework. Rangi drifted over to the Fiction shelves.

The books had little pictures on the spines – hearts, guns, space-ships, cowboys, magnifying glasses... You could tell at a glance what sort of story you were getting. Cool. He'd get himself a good detective novel and find out how to do it har har, as Sir would say.

The fattest book with a magnifying glass logo was *The Adventures of Sherlock Holmes*. Great. Rangi had really enjoyed the television series, and this guy was a classic. Lots of reading, too.

It was heavy going to start with, not all that much action. And Holmes really had the wrong idea about women –

He never spoke of the softer passions, save with a gibe and a sneer. They were admirable things for the observer – excellent for drawing the veil from men's motives and actions. But for the trained reasoner to admit such intrusions into his own delicate and finely adjusted temperament was to introduce a distracting factor which might throw a doubt upon all his mental results.

...Rangi's women never upset *his* delicate and finely adjusted temperament.

The old-fashioned language was quite easy once you got the hang of it. Restful, even. Besides, remembering the television series helped. Rangi kept chuckling as he read, thinking what Sir would say if he had Holmes on his team. What Holmes would make of Sir, come to that.

He took the book to bed with him fairly early. Clean sheets, smooth bed. He'd make a real effort and do the bed as soon as he got up every morning. And the dishes. There weren't enough to be worth washing tonight, but.

...He'd been "reading" the words for some time without actually taking anything in. Tired. It was a shit of a job. If he could be like Holmes, picking up the little details, putting them together... Super-sleuth har har. He switched the light off – listen to it; still pissing down. Detective Senior Sergeant Rangi Roberts pulled the blankets high, turned onto his side, tucked one hand between his knees, the other under the pillow, and slept, soothed by the drumming of the rain and the splattering of the water from the blocked guttering.

He woke early in grey morning and pulled the curtain aside to check the day. The window was streaked with rain, heavy clouds hung low over the trees. No work today. He stretched, the coverings warm around him. Another thing about a properly made bed – it didn't come apart in the middle of the night so that you woke early and freezing with the sheet wrapped round your throat. Cup of tea? Not yet. He switched on the light and reached for his book.

Holmes was a bloody marvel – that thing about the guy's hat, how much he could tell from just looking at it. His wife had stopped loving him, eh? Hell, it'd be something if women brushed guys' hats every morning these days. No one wore hats, anyway. This must've been a top hat sort of thing – with elastic under the chin (or at least it had *had* elastic under the chin). Jeez, if Rangi saw a bloke with his hat tied on with elastic he'd reckon he was a dork, not someone who was careful about property. He read on, but underneath he was unsettled. Holmes lived in a time when people did expected things – there was somehow a way you could tell a lot from people then by just little signs. Not like today... Rangi considered what sort of things he might be able to tell about people nowadays if they were a bit unusual, and sighed. He reckoned everyone was a bit unusual.

But if... if, for example, he saw a guy whose right arm was more sunburnt than his left, he could work out that he'd been driving his car a lot. With the window open, see. Hey, if it was the *left* arm that was sunburnt and not the right, then he'd know the guy had been overseas – America or Europe where they drove on the other side! He could just see Pike's face (Pike *was* a sort of Dr Watson, eh) when Rangi asked a guy if he'd had a good trip abroad.

But with Rangi's luck it'd probably turn out that the guy hadn't left the country, but had broken his leg so that it was his wife that drove him round during their summer holidays and his left arm was browner because he'd been in the passenger seat.

He read on until he heard footsteps passing his window. Not bloody visitors! He cautiously pulled the curtain aside, at least the weather seemed to be clearing. No visitors – just the guy next door out getting his mail. Shit! Was that the time already? He'd better stop lazing round and get himself something to eat. Then spend a quiet afternoon with a few beers watching whatever match happened to be on tv.

Later he went out to his own letterbox. He hadn't cleared it for a day or two and had been aware that junk mail and freebie newspapers were piling up, getting soggier by the day. Mum had missed that, too, same as the cobweb.

No bills, which was something. He took the mushy pile of circulars and advertising papers into the carport and opened the lid of the nearest bin. They were both his now, eh. He used the wad in his hand to squash the contents down so that there was room for more. As he pushed it into place, a stamp caught his eye. An Aussie stamp. Jeez, there was a letter in there – who'd be writing to him from Australia? Jim? Wasn't Jim living near Sydney now? He peeled the wet papers away.

Typical – it wasn't even for him. Typewritten address, Joseph Bradley, Flat 2... Bloody posties couldn't read. Well, Joseph Bradley must be the joy germ next door. Rangi was buggered if he was going to go round and hand it over personally. He'd just shove it back in the guy's box and he could find it tomorrow.

But the rain had stopped, and the envelope was not only sodden but had smears of printers ink from being next to soaking newsprint. Tomorrow this Joseph Bradley could well reason that, as the envelope in the letterbox was wet even though it hadn't rained since the previous mail delivery, the big goof next door had found it in his mail and hadn't had the decency to deliver it by hand. Elementary, my dear Pike.

Rangi set off down the path to Joseph Bradley's back door. Maybe he wouldn't be home.

But he was. The blue eyes were not friendly. "I *am* working."

"Found this in my mail. Reckon it's yours?"

The guy didn't take it straight away, just looked at it with distaste. Well, Rangi wasn't going to apologise for the weather.

"I –" Joseph Bradley began, and then he pushed his glasses down

and ducked his head to peer over them at the address. "Why, yes."
A skinny hand grabbed at the envelope. "Yes, it is mine. Thank you."
The rash on his face stood out redly. "Thank you very much. Most
kind." Now the face had flushed to the same tone as the rash. The
small mouth attempted a smile of farewell.

"No problem," said Rangi. "Sorry it's wet. Got mixed up in my
junk mail."

"That's quite all right." The door began to edge shut. Rangi leaned
against the porch wall, preparing for a neighbourly chat. There was
the primp of a smile again. "Quite understandable," Joseph Bradley
said. "Now I really must be –"

"Reckon I'll have a go at those leaves in the guttering," said Rangi,
who had started to enjoy himself. Whatever this letter was, the guy
was burning to get at it. "You haven't got a ladder, have you?"

"*I* managed perfectly well with a kitchen chair." The berk was
actually moving from one foot to another, almost hopping in his
impatience. "And you are considerably taller than I."

"Yeah," said Rangi, and as the door began to move again, he
nodded at the letter. "Got friends in Oz, eh?"

"In –? No. I've – ah – a correspondent, that's all."

"Yeah." Rangi rubbed a shoulder against the wall. "Not being
nosy, of course, just I saw the stamps and thought for a moment it
was a mate of mine. Good job I read the address first, eh."

"Most fortunate. Look, I –"

"Would've opened it otherwise. Thinking it was Jim, you see."

"Never mind, you didn't." But there had definitely been a nervous
glance at the seal. Rangi was pleased. Sherlock Holmes lives again.

"He's in Sydney."

"Who?"

"Jim. This mate of mine I was telling you about."

"Goodness me. Well, thank you again." This time the door shut
firmly.

Not that it compensated for a trip into the shops and forty dollars
on a new rubbish bin, but Rangi felt a good deal better. He returned
to his flat, fetched the kitchen steps and a plastic bag to put the leaves
in then went whistling to work on the guttering.

Joseph Bradley pushed the snib up on the back door with relief, and
went into the poky little lounge where he took the charming silver
Edwardian letter opener from the container beside his computer. Net

23

curtains shielded him from anyone who might be trying to peer in, but he stood well away from the window to be on the safe side. He had already checked the sender's address. It *was* from Frederick Tapper. His hands, he noted with annoyance, were shaking as he slit open the soggy envelope.

The paper was so wet he had to peel it carefully open. He read the letter over and then re-read it, reliving with amusement the disappointment that he had felt at the opening paragraph and his relief – his excitement – at the rest of the message. ...*writers of high calibre*. He'd known he was, of course. He knew that he was getting there. But for *Frederick Tapper* to say so...! Frederick Tapper was interested in his work! They would be working together on his – Joseph Bradley's – novels.

They would, of course, become friends. Close acquaintances. If Frederick Tapper died early, Joseph Bradley could well become the official biographer – people would acknowledge him as a confidant of the great man. And a writer of high calibre in his own right.

No one, but no one – Frederick was quite right – must know yet what was in the wind. Joseph Bradley would burst upon the literary world with perfect novels. He savoured in advance the petty jealousy, the resentful envy of the rest of the English Faculty. This was a better way, a much better way, of getting his own back for all the cheap insults, the slights, the functions to which he was not invited, the way he was ignored at those he did attend. It was a much better way than...

He must collect the other manuscripts and get them off to the post today. And – he glanced at his watch – he had a class at two p.m. He had to rush.

But he'd read the letter just once more.

One last thing. Might I suggest that you continue to keep your ambitions, and your writing, secret at this stage?

Well, there was no need to tell him that; secrecy was the name of the game, as the saying went, in Joseph Bradley's life right now. One of the conditions of his taking this flat was that the agents would not reveal where he was living. He had worried about the Jaguar – it was such a distinctive car – but he had not been able to bring himself to give up that atmosphere of old leather and luxury. Besides, his side of the carport was well shielded from view by the trees at the end of the driveway, the area was not one that university staff were likely to pass through, and he always took the precaution of driving a different way home. He knew They were watching, but was certain that so far no one had ever actually followed him. No one knew where Joseph Bradley was living now.

Except for the foolish macho type who lived next door. *He* knew all right – he'd seen the name on the envelope. Joseph Bradley's head was suddenly tight. That big Maori – he'd have looked at the return address, too. He'd know who Joseph Bradley's correspondent was! Something would have to be done about that. He collected a plastic bag from the kitchen and put the letter and envelope carefully inside so that it would not wet anything else. He pulled out a drawer of his desk and tucked the letter under spare paper. Then he went outside.

Clearing the guttering was a mucky job, but not unpleasant, and it didn't take all that long. Rangi was just shifting the steps so that he could reach the last bit when the neighbour came round the side of the house. Rangi nodded, expecting the guy to go straight on, but he didn't. He cleared his throat and waited till Rangi was paying attention. He had something to say.

"About the letter which you so kindly delivered," he began.

"Yeah?"

"You must, I assume, have read my name on the envelope."

What was this guy? Of course he'd read the bloody name. Rangi set down the steps. "Yeah. How I knew it was yours, eh."

"I would be grateful –" The blue eyes behind the glasses abruptly popped. Rangi turned in the direction of his neighbour's stare. A police car had turned into the drive.

"I'll speak to you about the matter later," said Joseph Bradley, and he turned, scuttling back down the path.

One of the new uniformed kids was driving. Pike got out of the passenger's side. He was carrying a folder and Rangi's heart sank. "What's all this?" he asked. "It's my day off."

"Nothing, Sarge. Just the reports from yesterday. You forgot to sign them, so I thought I'd drop round to see if you had a moment."

Good old Pike. He was a nice kid – Rangi had been put off to start with by that dreadful private school way of speaking, the stunning blond good looks. But for all his family's megabucks, Pike was the genuine article. They were becoming good mates. "Thanks. I'll just finish this and then get cleaned up and do them." He climbed the steps, scooped up the last mucky handful and took the bag of debris round to the rubbish bins.

"Time for a cuppa?" he asked.

"Well..." Pike glanced over his shoulder at the car.

"Tell him to come in too. What's his name?"

"Burns. Chaddie Burns."

"Out you get, Burns." Rangi nodded towards the driver. "Bit of r and r."

Once inside, Rangi told them to make themselves at home. "You can put the jug on, Pike, while I go and wash."

Ashley Pike hadn't been inside Sarge's place before. It was really tiny, but neat and smart as a new pin. The only mess was a few dishes still in the sink. There was even a rose in a little vase on the kitchen table. Ashley collected cups, saucers, coffee and sugar from gleaming, well-ordered kitchen cupboards. The milk stood in a spotless, fragrant fridge. No crumbs in the cutlery drawer the way there were in Ashley's apartment.

Sarge came in before Ashley had finished, but he didn't elbow in and try to take over. "Doing a good job there, man," he said. "There's cheese biscuits in the tin on top of the fridge." And he took the folder of reports through into the lounge to sign. They couldn't talk much about work with Chaddie there, and Ashley couldn't stay long anyway. But it was great to be sitting just chatting about the weather and rugby and that. Sarge was more like a friend than his boss, and he made fantastic biscuits. You never knew how people lived, they always surprised you. Ashley took another cheese buster. The thought of Sarge baking them...

Ashley and Chaddie washed up – Ashley insisted; he didn't want Sarge to think he was a slob. Then they left. "Thanks again," Sarge said as he saw them to the door. "Sir would've had my guts for garters if he'd seen the things unsigned." His grin warmed Ashley all the way back to work.

The neighbour was at Rangi's back door a minute or so after Pike and Burns had left. "I do hope there is nothing wrong?" he began.

"Wrong?"

"No... bad news or anything."

"No. Why?"

"Well, the police car... You..."

"Oh that. Nah. Just one of the guys bringing a bit of work round."

The blue eyes popped again. "You're... you're in the police force? But you don't..."

"Wear uniform? No, those days are over. I'm a detective."

"Oh." The guy's eyes swivelled to the side. "Goodness me. That must be an interesting occupation."

"Mostly paper work. Mostly dead boring." Hey, he'd really impressed the bugger. Rangi drew himself up and smiled in self deprecation. "Actually."

"Oh." You could tell he was wanting to leave. Feet shuffling round again. Why the hell had he come, then? Wanting to find out what sort of bother his unsavoury neighbour had got himself into? Sticking that long, wandering nose into a bit of hot gossip? If he'd thought Rangi was in trouble, the truth must really have rocked him.

"Well," said Rangi, "what can I do for you?"

"Oh – ah – nothing really. A most trivial matter. I won't bother you with it."

"No. Come on." Nice to see him on the back foot like this.

"It's just – that letter..."

"Yeah...?"

"It's a silly thing, really. I have let my own house – temporarily – and am living here so that... so that I can have some privacy, you understand..."

Well, dropping in for chats with the next-doors wasn't a very good way of going about that.

"I would be very grateful – you read my name on the envelope, of course – very grateful if you would not mention to anyone that I was living here."

"Why should I?"

"Of course, why should you? However, it might just come into conversation – you might just mention that you had a new neighbour and drop my name in, as it were... and... and I'd rather you didn't." The face was bright scarlet now.

"I'll bear it in mind," said Rangi. Then Holmes prompted, "This privacy, you want... Any particular reason?"

"Oh, nothing. Just... just... I am working on something that really does not lend itself to constant interruptions, and... where I was known, there was, of course, a constant flow of visitors."

There was, was there? And the guy's eyes had moved to the side again. He was lying. Not the popular type, Rangi reckoned.

"Anyway." The mouth was trembling as it tried to smile. "Anyway,

27

I must get back to work again, and not waste your time by chatting. Nice to have met you."

"See you round," said Rangi, but the guy was already half-way down the path. He shut the door, thinking hard. What would Holmes have made of all that?

Joseph Bradley had been dreadfully shocked to see the police car nosing its way into the drive.

And the tenant next door was... not only a policeman, but a *detective*... There was a sudden drumming in his temples – was there any possibility that the estate agent had been primed to show Joseph this flat where he would be under the constant eye of the law?... His Enemies were not altogether fools; They could well have realised that he suspected They were following him to his house and that he was likely to decide to change his address. And the flat, though unattractive enough in itself, had been very reasonable. Had it been too reasonable? Was someone subsidising his rent?

If that were the case, the estate agency must be party to it. Joseph thought things through. It was not only possible. It was probable. Well, They'd find that he was more than a match for Them.

But now he was in a rush. He had barely time to pack up the manuscripts of his other novels and get them to the post before his lecture. He had not finished writing the long letter to Frederick Tapper yesterday evening. The business with the rubbish bin had been too upsetting. So for now he simply typed a brief covering note: *Other mss, as requested. Letter follows. JB.*

Although posted later, the promised letter from Joseph Bradley arrived before the packet of manuscripts. It was a brilliantly clear autumn day and Frederick walked in the garden as he read it. He had, for the time being, given up all pretence of work. Perhaps if he gave himself a proper break, he'd get back into the swing of things easily.

God, the man was a bore! What a screed of academic drivel. How the hell had this dork produced *The Pungent Collection*? But at least he'd swallowed the bait – hook, line and sinker. Joseph would respect Frederick's request for secrecy, was most grateful that Frederick considered his work worthy of attention, blah blah.

Frederick thought he could probably spin the correspondence out for six months or so, tinkering with *The Pungent Collection* and the other works which were on their way. Perhaps he should suggest his apprentice start on another novel, sending him each chapter for critical analysis before moving on to the next. That should delay things for at least a year. And if Frederick still had nothing on the way by then – well, it would be... it was bloody unthinkable, that was all. Nausea welled up in his throat.

The large packet of manuscripts arrived the following day. Frederick took it into his office and tore off the wrapping. He started with the latest work, a novel entitled *Automobiles and Knickknacks*. It wasn't very long – shorter than *The Pungent Collection*. Frederick finished it after lunch and sat for a while in stunned despair.

All the novels were good. He read one a day, becoming more and more depressed. It was as though the thing that moved *his* mind had simply deserted him to take up lodgings with this pompous twerp. Well, there was nothing for it, he'd have to start his delaying tactics then and there. It wasn't going to be easy. How *could* he find fault with work which so closely resembled his own?

He left it to the next day and then began the first of the letters that was to become, all that autumn and winter, a long dreary correspondence with Joseph Bradley.

 three

All that autumn and winter, Joseph Bradley, despite his Enemies, was happier than he had been in years. He had considered changing where he lived once more, but realised that if They had "nobbled" the estate agents once, They would only do so again. In any case, he had more important things on his mind. He hugged his secret to him, content to wait until the time when his work sprang upon an amazed world. He and Frederick Tapper were working together on a novel that he was writing. *Myself When Old* was the working title. Chapter after chapter he sent across the Tasman, chapter after chapter came back with subtle suggestions, careful analyses. Joseph wrote long replies detailing his reactions to the suggestions. Their very correspondence was becoming a thing of art.

Despite the need for secrecy about his writing, Joseph had applied for membership of the recently formed local branch of the national authors' group. As he pointed out to Frederick in an early letter, there was no danger that any member would want to chat about Joseph's work; they were all far too busy posturing about their own. In fact, Joseph never once said anything at any of the monthly meetings (Joseph considered monthly swill would be a more appropriate term), but sat silent while gossip and intrigue fluttered about him. The evenings had proved a rich source of material, and his attendance had the added piquancy of his knowledge that soon, *soon*, when the novels of Joseph Bradley were taking the world by storm, the pretentious condescension of the "full" members would be shown for what it was.

The term "full" members afforded Joseph grim amusement as he watched the monthly tanking-up. At the same time it rankled – when he had applied for membership he had been welcomed – *welcomed*! – as an "Associate Member." The Secretary had explained that only those who had published work could be awarded "full" membership.

This twittery poof whose one claim to authorship was a collection of banal verse published some years previously had had the gall to imply that he, Joseph Bradley, was not a "proper" writer.

Joseph had considered telling the limp-wristed degenerate what he could do with his "Associate Membership," but had finally decided to swallow his pride for the moment. The Secretary was a teacher at a local secondary school, and not long after Joseph's acceptance of "Associate Membership" the school's Board of Trustees had received an anonymous letter suggesting that the Secretary's interest in some of his pupils was unhealthy, to say the least. It was suggested that his activities in the drama club he ran would repay investigation. Joseph had noted with satisfaction the signs of stress which the Secretary had shown over the last year.

All that autumn and winter, other members of the branch, guilty of slighting Joseph by ignoring him utterly or by their patronising attitudes as evidenced in their frequent and obvious efforts to include him in conversations or to fill his glass, were seeming increasingly strained as well...

Few of those whose family or employers had received anonymous letters knew for certain who was resonsible, but some did. For lack of proof, perhaps, or through the apathy that can come from misery, however, they took no action. But those who did know and who still had to do with Bradley shunned him, and their distaste for his company influenced those around him. He became more and more isolated; isolation in turn increased his paranoia and the number of letters.

Still nothing was done. Even the father of young Robby Hale, whose death was the direct result of Bradley's letter to the University Council, did nothing.

From the day after Robby's death, when his letter to his parents had arrived, Bob Hale had ferreted around until he learnt enough to know he had the truth.

Robby's letter had not stressed anyone's guilt but his own – and his own despair. Poor little Robby, he'd always been the same. He'd do anything for his friends, promise them the earth and then be in despair when it came time to deliver. Bob and Brenda had pulled him out of scrapes often enough. The sheepish introduction of the mate from primary school, from high school, from university; the tug on

31

the arm in the privacy of the kitchen; the desperate whisper, *I told him you'd give him ten dollars... Dad, I thought your suit might fit Alistair, he hasn't got one for the senior ball... If you're not doing much tomorrow, I wondered if you'd mind driving Mike down to Palmerston – he sort of thinks you're going down there anyway.*

And though there were recriminations and frequent promises that Robby would stop "using" his parents like this, well... well he *was* their only one, eh? And a bloody good one at that. Look how he'd flown through the academic world – no one from the whole family had ever dreamt of university before, but Robby – only straight from finishing his Masters into a Junior Lectureship while he worked on his Doctorate! That's all. Doctor Hale, he was going to be. Doctor Robert Hale.

And the boy had never been stuck up, never snobby about all his learning, never ashamed that his Dad was just Bob Hale of Hale's Garage. A good son, a good boy – fond of his parents and never – apart from him being over-generous – never any trouble. And when you think how much trouble others had with teenage boys... Brenda doted on him.

But then, it seemed, Robby had promised a friend something that he really shouldn't have promised. The friend had got a good pass on the paper Robby had marked, and all would have been well if there hadn't been some sick bugger who'd written off to the University Council. Insinuating all sorts of warped things – not only about the mark, but hinting that this friend – a man friend – had been Robby's... Bob saw red. There was nothing wrong with his boy. He'd had girlfriends a plenty. Looking like that, of course he had.

But the gossip and the smearing – and the dread of the coming investigation – had got to Robby in a weak moment and he'd... Bob's mind veered away to the funeral, to the sympathy of two of Robby's mates, Jones and Hancock – university types, but genuinely sorry, really full of concern – for Brenda especially. They'd let drop that they had their suspicions about the letter writer; he hadn't taken them up on it then and there – the wrong time and the wrong place – but he'd caught up with them later, and they'd told him all they knew.

Which was quite a bit. They'd both been recently separated from their partners as a result of anonymous letters. One true, one not. ("Doesn't matter which was which," Hancock grinned.) They'd compared notes, realised that some other members of the staff showed signs of strain, asked a few questions, got fewer answers – but they got some. They worked out dates, realised that the letters had started a short time after Bradley's appointment to the staff.

They had friends at Victoria University. They'd checked with them. A steady vitriolic trickle of anonymous letters that had afflicted Victoria had dried up the instant Bradley had left the staff. They were certain in their own minds.

"Proof's another thing," said Jones. "All we can do is warn people at the moment – and then only in general terms, unless we're certain of who we're talking to. That bastard would get us for libel – and love doing it."

"But you've got a right to know," Hancock added. "After poor Robert's death..."

"Yeah," Bob said. "And I really appreciate you telling me like this. What I needed to know, eh." They shook his hand, patted his arm – there was no side about these guys at all. Good blokes, both of them.

For a while he watched Bradley. Not all the time – he still put in a fair day's work at the workshop most days. But he got to know Bradley's face, got to know his movements – followed him a few times as Bradley drove his bloody roundabout way back to his flat. The flat seemed an odd place for a guy with a pay-packet like his to be living in.

At night Bob would dream of Robby's face – fresh, hopeful, loving – alongside the closed, self-satisfied smirk of Bradley. The bastard actually came into the workshop once while Bob was there. Hale's wasn't his regular garage, but he'd had a puncture right across the road. He had light blue eyes that stuck out behind thick lensed glasses. His nose meandered all over his pale prissy face and he had a mouth like a girl. A skinny maggot with a sort of rash under the skin of his cheeks. Bob held his hands tightly behind his back as he listened to the thin, whining voice making its demands of young Phillipson. Finally, he turned away, trembling. He went home early.

Of course, he did nothing. What was there to do? And having once seen his son's murderer (it *had* been murder) close up, he lost his taste for dogging him around.

All that autumn and winter, Rangi struggled to impress Sir. He managed one or two quite good things; since he'd read *Sherlock Holmes* he'd made a real effort to notice little details. It did seem to pay off.

All that autumn and winter, Julia, Frederick Tapper's devoted agent, wrote, faxed and telephoned with solicitous enquiries about the novel in progress and Frederick Tapper continued blandly reassuring.

During that autumn and winter Frederick Tapper came to hate Joseph Bradley with a deep and deadly loathing.

And then, one spring morning, Julia turned up unannounced at Frederick's door. "I had to come over anyway," she said, "and I simply couldn't resist taking a couple of extra days to hire a car, pop across and see how you were getting on." They embraced – a ceremony Julia had instigated, and one that Frederick could well do without.

"You'll stay the night?" Frederick had to ask her, of course. It would seem rude not to, she'd smell a rat, the sharp bitch.

"If you'll have me." Julia managed, as usual, to slide a secondary meaning under her words. She should be so lucky! Frederick smiled politely.

They had coffee standing in the kitchen while Julia prattled on about how the filming was going – she'd visited the shoot just before leaving New Zealand. As she rinsed her coffee mug, she said, "And now – let's see what you've got for me. You've been very naughty this time not even letting me have a peek so that I can start titillating the publishers. I'm thinking about an auction for this one, and I can't do that, can I, if I don't know a little about what's up for grabs?"

And Frederick Tapper heard himself say, "You can have more than a peek. You can have the whole thing."

"It's *finished*?"

"It's finished," said Frederick's voice.

"You wicked man! I didn't have a clue!" Julia did a quick soft shoe shuffle and made as if to embrace Frederick.

Frederick stepped quickly backwards. "Go and sit outside on the deck." He tried to make his mouth smile naturally. "I'll bring it out."

In his office, he sorted through the manuscripts, found *The Pungent Collection*, removed the title page – thank God Bradley hadn't put his name on each sheet – and took it out to Julia.

"Untitled? We'll have to do something about that. I'll need a title to dicker with."

"Read it first. We can think of a title when you've finished."

Julia looked up as she finished reading the first page. "Oh, wondrous man! You've done it again, haven't you?"

"Yes," said Frederick. "I've done it, I think. I've really done it this time."

She read on. The housekeeper brought their lunch outside and afterwards Frederick went for a long walk. He couldn't stand Julia's appreciative giggles. When he got back she'd finished the whole thing. Her eyes were shining. "It's wonderful! Superb!" He suffered her embrace. "It's far and away your best yet."

"No it isn't!"

His vehemence startled her, but she simply gave his shoulders a little squeeze. "False modesty, Freddie? That's not like you." She left her hands on his shoulders and moved closer.

"Why don't you go and get your luggage while I get us both a drink?" he said. "Your usual room's made up." The whipped puppy look in her eyes again. Would the silly bitch never learn? Frederick Tapper was not interested in any woman – or any man, if it came to that. Even the urgency of youth had left him almost unscathed.

Julia was an damn good agent, though. Wily as a fox and steel hard when it came to business dealings. He'd once told her, as she gave him an account of the negotiations over a radio play, that he was bloody glad she was on his side. He was, too. He mixed her a gin and made himself a Pernod, being careful not to drown it.

Why the hell had he done it? He could have stalled her for longer – even confessed he was having a dry patch. He felt sick. When she came back in she was carrying an armload of bottles. "Duty free," she said. "And I brought you some of that Marlborough white you were so keen on. Mrs Whatnot's put it in the fridge."

"That's decent of you." He handed her the gin.

"I only wish I'd brought some bubbly. We've really got something to celebrate."

"Oh, I dunno." He sat down. "About this one... I don't want it to come out too soon, you know?"

"You *what*! Freddie, I tell you here and now that I'll be shooting it all over the place as soon as I can get the copies run off. That book is auction material, if ever I saw it. It's – it's... well, you *must* know how good it is."

"Shut up, Julia. No, the thing is that I don't feel it's really ready. I got to fiddle with it a bit more, you know?" His Pernod had disappeared. "Another?" he asked.

"Still going, thanks. And you keep your hands off that script. It is perfect as it is."

"I think *I* am the best judge of that, don't you?" He saw her flinch at the ice in his voice. But that was the answer – he could tell her he was still working on it; then later he'd say that he'd scrapped the whole thing. Throw an artistic tantrum when she flipped. He'd delay things until he had something of his own to show her.

Something of his own...bloody hell – *It's far and away your best yet*. The bitch had no judgement, no bloody judgement at all.

He drew himself up in his chair. "You've read this draft," he said. "And don't forget it's only a draft. I let you read it so you can talk to publishers. But I am not, I repeat *not*, really satisfied with it yet and so I'm not going to let you take it when you go – I'll let you know when I think it's properly finished. And for Christ's sake, don't tell anyone what it's about."

"Why not?"

"Never you bloody mind why not. You're keen on it, that's great. Let them see you think it's terrific, but don't tell them anything more."

She was stunned. "But they'll want to know more – they *need* to know more. Look, just let me have it and I'll tell them it's only a draft, okay? Freddie, for pity's sake."

But he played stubborn and eventually she subsided. They got through the rest of the day without Julia's making any more advances, without the least hint of *double entendre* in her conversation. Frederick drank heavily and went early to bed. If she hadn't been such a tough cookie, he'd have thought she was going to weep when he said goodnight.

She left early the next morning. Frederick, nursing a gargantuan hangover, shuffled out in his dressing gown to say goodbye. She kissed him reproachfully and went. He headed back to bed for the day. He'd been an idiot, but at least it was over with.

But it wasn't. One evening a week later he was sitting in front of the fire with the whisky bottle beside him when the doorbell trilled. For a while he thought it was the television – he hadn't been watching the show, it was just there for company – but the insistent noise finally shook him out of his blackness and he went to the door.

Julia. Julia standing there, with her case, a couple of bottles of bubbly and a tentative smile. "I thought I'd better apologise," she said, handing him the bottles. "May I stay? I can go to a motel if you'd rather."

Like hell she was here to apologise. She was here to have another go. He took the bottles. Vintage. "Mi' swell come in." He was alarmed that his voice was so slurred. "Come in," he said more carefully. "Come in by the fire and chew on y'r bone."

"I shouldn't have tried to bully you," she said. She did actually settle on the hearth rug, her hands out to the flames. He managed to get glasses out of the cabinet and open the first bottle. "You were quite right, Freddie. You do know your work best. And I'll just have to wait patiently until you're ready for me."

With extreme caution he carried the foaming glasses across the room. He handed her one and then pointed at her, "Stay!" he said, and giggled.

"Thanks so much." Her voice was puzzled. "I was hoping I could, like I said."

"Shtay!" This time he joggled his glass as he pointed. "Bugger," he said. "Waste of good wine."

"It's only a little bit. I'll get a cloth." She put her glass down and stood up.

"Sure you don' wanna lick it up?"

"You're pissed, Freddie." She looked at him as he slumped back in his chair. "Really pissed." She disappeared into the kitchen and came back with paper towels. "Are you drinking a lot these days?" she asked as she mopped up the carpet and threw the towels onto the fire where they sizzled and flared.

"Not pissed. Just... sad."

"Oh, poor Freddie. What's the matter, then?" She shuffled towards him on her knees and leant against one arm of his chair. It was as much as he could do not to pat her head.

"Nothing's the matter. Bloody nothing's the matter. Top this up, will you?"

"Do you think you should have any more? I'd never have suggested it if I'd realised..."

"Just bloody top it up. Do what you're told." He sensed uncomfortably that she enjoyed his ordering her around, even if he was... even if he had been drinking a bit. She got up obediently and refilled his glass. Then she sat on the floor and leant against his knees. Taking advantage. She would.

"Something's the matter. This isn't like you. You can tell me, even if you can't tell anyone else."

And he told her. He bloody opened his mouth and told her. At the end of it all, she was kneeling there with her arms around him and he was fucking well crying on her shoulder.

"It was a silly, silly thing to do, Freddie, but you had every excuse. You're really stressed out, my darling. And you mustn't worry about not working. Of course you'll work again. You're Frederick Tapper." Even in this state, he winced at the note of reverence as she said his name. She got out a tissue and mopped his tears – the room was twirling round and he felt he was going to chuck fairly soon. If she kissed him again, he'd chuck right then and there and serve her right.

But she didn't kiss him again. He saw her face spinning close towards him and then it was gone and he felt her hands on his arms, pulling him up. "Come on," she said. "I'm going to put you to bed. We'll talk about this in the morning."

"Mange perfec' well. Put m'self to bed, thank you ver' mush." He squinted across the room trying to get the door to stay in one place, took a step and then the floor came up and hit him. It came right up and hit him.

He woke in the late morning, his head near bursting. He was in bed wearing just his briefs. The light, when he opened his eyes a crack, was jagged and painful. He shut his eyes. What the hell had happened last night?

He carefully tiptoed round his memory. Julia. She'd turned up. A picture of her, elegant, trying for cosy cuteness as she stretched her hands out towards the fire. God, he'd hung one on! What had he done? What had he said?

...Oh fuck... Oh shit... Oh hell and damnation and... Oh Christ... He'd...

No wonder he'd drunk so much. And her... He opened his eyes cautiously, blinking against the pain. It was his own bed he was in. He slowly turned his head. The other side of the bed was undisturbed, the pillow smooth. He released a long breath. Thank the powers for small mercies!

But all the same, even if she hadn't taken advantage of his drunkenness, she sure as hell would get her money's worth out of this one. God, he'd have to face her sometime today. Her, knowing all that. He groaned.

And as on cue, there was a tap on the door and she peeked in. Had she been sitting on the mat outside his room waiting for her master's voice?

"How are you, Freddie? Are you all right?"

"Fine," he mumbled. "Just fine. What's the time?"

She came and perched on the side of his bed, put a cool hand on his forehead. "Poor love," she said. "What a terrible time you've been having."

He made himself smile at her. "I was an idiot last night," he said. "Sorry."

"Oh, Freddie, darling Freddie, don't apologise. *I'm* the one who should apologise. I should have come over more often – heaven knows I wanted to – should have seen that things were wrong before you got yourself into this state... Can I get you a cup of tea? Aspirin?"

Well, let her wait on him if that's what she wanted. He could do with it right now. "Coffee," he said. "And there's aspirin in the bathroom cabinet."

"Two?"

"Three. What's the time?"

"Nearly lunchtime. Mrs Thingummy is getting it now. Would you like yours in bed?"

"I'll get up."

"Good. It's a lovely day – we can eat outside where we can talk."

Of course they'd bloody have to talk. He sighed. "You know, I can't remember getting to bed."

"I'm not surprised. You'd passed out." She went into the bathroom.

"How did I get here then?"

"I managed."

"You *carried* me? But-"

"I may be skinny, but I'm fit," she said. "Here. Aspirin."

He lifted his head as he held out his hand for the pills and the glass of water. "Jesus!" he groaned.

"Poor Freddie. I'll get the coffee. And the papers and your mail." A light kiss on the forehead and she scampered out of the room.

"Just the coffee," he called after her, his voice rumbling around his head. "I don't think my eyes are up to reading yet."

A scalding hot shower worked with the coffee and aspirin to make him feel a little more like a human being. He scrubbed at his teeth, dressed, found his dark glasses, and went into the living room.

"Out here, Freddie," she called from the balcony. Lunch was already on the table.

As he sat, she stood up and went to the sliding doors. "Your Mrs Thing said she was going to do your room," she said, "but I'll shut these just in case."

Here it came, the long earnest tête-à-tête where she demonstrated her loyalty and understanding.

But he'd underestimated her. "This Joseph Bradley," she said, "has he got an agent?"

God, that was cool. That was bloody cool. Off with the old and on with the new, was it? Frederick Tapper is dead, long live Joseph Bradley, future star in the stable of Julia Whitehead.

And how much had Frederick told her last night? He could only remember bits. "No," he said. "He hasn't got an agent. I'll give you his address if you like."

"Freddie! What are you thinking? *One* writer like you is as much as a girl could hope for."

"Well, he's a writer like me – you said that bloody book was the best yet. And I'm no longer a writer. So why not?"

"Now, just you stop that. Wallowing in self pity! You're hung over. You'll be writing again."

She was enjoying herself. She had always loved finding little things to tick him off about and this time she'd be having a field day.

"I asked if he had an agent for a very good reason. Now. Who apart from you has seen his work?"

"No one."

"*No one*? Are you sure?"

He started to nod and then thought better of it. "Sure I'm sure. I'll show you some of his letters and you'll see why. The man's mad. Paranoid, I'd say. Persecution complex, relates everything to himself, and he's extremely secretive. How the hell he ever manages to turn out work like that..."

"Freddie, I've been thinking... It's..." She'd started confidently, but now she hesitated, her eyes all over the place. She tried another tack. "How long do you think this dry spell is going to last?"

"How the hell can I tell. Forever? It feels like forever. It's been long enough now."

A sympathetic hand reached over his. He coughed in order to take his hand away and search for a handkerchief. God, his head hurt; coughing had not been a good thing to do.

"You said his other novels are just about as good as this one..."

"Yeah." What the hell was she on about?

"And they're all... you could have written any one of them?"

"I said."

There was a pause.

"...You don't like him?"

"Never met him. But from his letters he's a... an atrocious person."
He hesitated and then added, "I hate the bugger."

"Of course you do. How old would you say he is?"

"What's that got to do with it?"

"Never mind just now. Any idea how old?"

"He sent me a cv early on. I'll have it somewhere."

"Tell me where it is and I'll get it."

"No." He didn't want her going through his things. "I'll get it. If
it's really important."

"It's important." He went into his office.

"Here you are," he said, putting the pages on the table.

She got up and shut the door again while she read. "Born 1942,"
she said. "Early fifties."

"So?"

"He's healthy, would you say?"

"Christ, Julia, what is this?"

"Not likely to keel over, leaving his unpublished works unknown?"

"Some hopes." There was wine in the carafe; he poured himself
a small hair of the dog.

She sighed. "Wouldn't it be lovely if he did! All those novels... that
could have been written by Frederick Tapper."

He sipped gingerly. "Yeah. All those novels."

"How many are there?"

"Five. Five of the buggers, counting *The Pungent Collection*."

"*The Pungent Collection*?"

"The one you've read."

"Oooh, what a title. It's perfect!"

Frederick sniffed, and she gave him a brief smile. "Five," she said.
"Your regular output is around one every eighteen months." She'd
stopped hesitating now, she was leading up to something. He put his
glass down and took a forkful of salad.

"So?"

"So... if they *were* novels by Frederick Tapper, they'd be enough
to last you nearly eight years. In eight years, surely, you'll be working
again."

"But," he said firmly, "they are *not* novels by Frederick Tapper.
Frederick Tapper is a had-it. Frederick Tapper might as well jump off
the nearest bloody bridge."

She hesitated then said, "I need to know how much it matters to

41

you – not that you're not writing, I know how you feel about that – but how much do you want the world not to *know* that you're not writing? How important is it to you that your books should continue to appear?"

"It's important."

"Really important?"

"Yes it's really bloody important. But it's not going to happen so will you stop worrying away at it, for fuck's sake!"

"Freddie, I'm going to suggest something that – well, if you don't like it, we'll just forget all about it, forget it was ever mentioned. I want you to promise that my suggesting it will make no difference to our relationship."

What was coming? He felt the chill of winter behind the warm spring sun. Shut her up now. Bang her across the snout with a rolled up newspaper. "Go on," said Frederick Tapper's voice.

"You promise?"

"That it won't make any difference? I promise. You're a bloody good agent."

"If this Joseph Bradley were knocked over in a hit and run accident or something, no one would think of murder."

"...God."

She shut her eyes and forged ahead, her voice low and rapid. "If you went over there – took him out to dinner to discuss his works, it'd give me a chance to get into his house, get the letters you sent him... He'll have kept them, I suppose?"

"Bound to."

"There's only the letters to connect you with him?"

"Only those and the fact that I'd be seen with him if I took him out to dinner – which I'm not going to do. People do know my face, you know – even over there."

"...Yes." Her eyes were open again, she frowned in thought. "But," her face cleared, "but you could leave the country after that. There'd be no need for an accident until you were safely ensconced back here. Until you were known to be back here."

"*You'd* do it?"

"Oh yes." Her eyes fixed him. "I'd do it... for you."

It was too much. Bile rose in his throat and he swallowed hard. "No," said Frederick Tapper. "No way. No."

"You mean, you wouldn't want me to put myself at risk?"

"I mean no. It's not on. It's bloody not on. The whole idea's insane.

We'll do like you said and just not think about it again. This whole conversation's wiped, okay?"

Her eyes hardened. "And you'll get back to work tomorrow then?"

"Tomorrow. Sometime. What the fuck? This, *this* we are not doing."

She sighed. "You've been playing him along, you know," she murmured. "He wouldn't like to know that. He'd be likely to tell the world if he knew you'd been holding his books back from publishing... wouldn't he?"

"Who'd tell him?"

"There's only one person who knows." She watched him while this registered.

"My God!"

"If I had to, I would. Tell him I've read one and offer my services as his agent."

There was nothing doggy about her now. Her eyes glinted like a cat's. He looked away from her and stared out over the garden. Her voice softened. "Freddie, I wouldn't want to. It's the last thing I'd want to do. But..."

He let it hang there. Watched a bird moving from branch to branch pecking into blossom, tilting its head, wary, alert.

She was remorseless. "You said yourself that he's a thoroughly obnoxious type. You hate him, don't you?"

There was a whirring of wings as the bird flew off. "How..." said Frederick Tapper slowly, "how do you reckon you could get into his house?"

four

Rangi walked round to the garage and picked up his car when he came off duty. "New muffler, squire," Mike said. "The other was bashed to bits, we couldn't weld her."

That bloody culvert. "You got any metal strips I can put over a gutter?" Rangi asked.

"That the trouble, is it? Thought it might be something like that. Let's see now." Mike's hands, stubby, competent, smeared with black oil (*This man, Watson, works with machinery.* Well, even Watson could've seen that) searched through junk on a workbench. "How'd this be?"

"Excellent."

"Just one? There's a couple here."

"I'll take them both if you can spare them."

"Not a problem."

Rangi pulled up opposite the flats and lugged the plates out. He would set them up before he drove inside, while it was still light enough to see. And then, no more scraping and bumping. It'd been months, and the bloody estate agents had done nothing about it. Last time he'd phoned them they'd apologised, but said they were having to undergo a massive tax investigation and that all papers – including notes from clients – had been taken by the IRD.

As he was closing the lid of the boot, a green car drove slowly towards him and pulled up opposite. The woman who was driving leant over, peering away from him towards the flats. Did he have a visitor? Sure as hell she wouldn't be after the guy next door – Rangi had seen no callers in all the months the prick had been there. He tucked one metal plate under each arm and crossed the road.

"Looking for someone?" he said as he neared the car. The woman turned, startled, and her window slid shut. (*She's pressed the wrong button, Watson, therefore this car does not belong to her.* That was a good one.) Her face through the darkened glass was lovely. Rangi, burdened as he was with the metal, couldn't gesture to her, but he nodded towards the window. She hesitated and then it slid open a little.

"Can I help?" he said. "Who is it you're wanting?"

"No," she said. "No, I don't think so. This is obviously the wrong address."

"That's cool." Rangi grinned. "Hoped you might be looking for me." (No harm in trying.) "What address did you want?"

But she wasn't interested – he hadn't seriously thought she would be. She smiled briefly. "I'll find it." The window slid shut again, and Rangi stepped back to let the car pull out.

Julia's hands were wet on the steering wheel as she drove down the street. Hell and damnation! Chatting to the guy who lived over the road from the flats was no way to hide the fact that there was any connection between her and Joseph Bradley. She turned a couple of corners and then pulled up to get herself together, nerve herself for another try.

She glanced at her watch. Freddie had promised her at least two hours, but it was already fifteen minutes since she'd seen Joseph Bradley's maroon Jaguar purring past her round the corner, its driver on his way to his dinner date with a famous author. She'd waited so long in case Bradley came back for something he'd forgotten.

She *had* to do it now. If she didn't manage to collect the letters, then the rest of the plan couldn't go ahead, and Freddie would be lost. The great Frederick Tapper, who was going to be utterly dependent on her, so thankful for her risk and her sacrifice that he would... show his gratitude in any way she demanded. Remember why you're doing this, she told herself. Just keep it in mind. It's worth it. Now stop being a mindless idiot and damn well get on with it.

It was getting dark fast now. This would make it harder to search for the spare key that everybody left somewhere in case of emergencies. On the other hand, it meant that neighbours would be less likely to notice someone pottering about outside Joseph Bradley's flat. Get going.

This time she left the hired car round the corner from the flats, and walked the rest of the way. Someone had already seen the car in the street – for it to appear again might arouse suspicion. Not that anyone was likely to notice, she realised. Lights were on in almost all the houses already, the street itself was deserted. There was no sign of the big Maori guy who lived opposite.

Flat 2 was the one further from the road. Good. Joseph Bradley's next-door neighbours were already at home, there were lights on and she could hear the television blaring as she walked past, her black sneakers making no noise on the path.

He'd left the back porch light on – he was the sort who'd be expecting burglars every night, of course. Damn. She turned back to look at the street. There were some trees which would shield her a little, but they were not yet in full leaf and anyone looking out from a house opposite would be sure to spot her. All the evening curtains were closed, though; she'd have to chance it. She pulled on a pair of black cotton gloves and, standing on tiptoe, just managed to reach the light bulb. Even through the gloves it was hot – she nearly dropped it as it came free. She carefully put it on the floor of the porch and then went round the windows of the flat first; one might be loose.

But the place was hermetically sealed. That figured. There were two doors; the "front" door was on the side opposite the back porch. To get it you had to walk right round the back of the flats – that entrance was not likely to be used very often. He hadn't thought to put the front light on, thank heavens. She returned and began a methodical search of the area around the back porch.

The moon was nearly full and as well as that a little light from a street lamp reached as far as the porch. There was, of course, nothing under the mat. She hadn't expected there to be. Carefully, despite her growing feeling of urgency – she glanced at her watch – God, she had an hour and a half at least yet, there was no need to get uptight – she lifted a carton of jars waiting for a glass collection. Nothing. One by one she took out the empty jars, checked inside, underneath. Nothing. She replaced them.

The porch had no other hiding places. No pot plants – she'd been hoping for pot plants. A stone in the garden?

There was a small herb garden just springing into life, beside the porch. She pushed plants aside, patted the earth. A tang of mint and thyme in the air, nothing on the ground. No stones.

The herbs were surrounded by a small concrete edging. She felt all round it. One section was cracked and loose. She had to use both hands to lift it. There was nothing underneath. She let it grit back into position.

46

The front door? She went silently round the flat and searched again. Fruitlessly. The carport then. God, what if his neighbours decided to go for a drive? But she'd hear a door, see lights, they'd turn the television off first.

There was one car there – the empty side must be his. She felt round the single wooden joist that ran along the wall. There was nothing on it, nothing taped below it.

Three rubbish bins stood beside the car, two filled to overflowing, the other, when she lifted it, light, almost empty. The concrete floor under it was clear. She tilted the bin. No key taped to the bottom. And nothing taped under the lid. She turned her attention to the full bins.

They were heavy – smelly. No one in their right mind would tape a key to the underside of those lids. She lifted each bin, checked underneath. Of course not. Bloody hell.

The letter box. Nothing. She looked at her watch. Only one hour left. *Where?*

She checked the trees that stood at the end of the drive, the others that lined the low fence, took off her gloves so that she could feel along the underside of branches, delve her fingers into knot holes.

Maybe the bastard didn't keep a spare key anywhere.

Or maybe he left it with his neighbours. Should she knock on their door, pretend she was his niece, anxious to get inside and surprise him when he got back?

Don't be bloody ridiculous. *No one* must see you.

Think. If you're secretive, suspicious, certain that They are watching your every move, what do you do about your spare house key?

You hide it, that's what you do. You hide it superbly well.

She rechecked the porch, noticed the simple white plastic light shade. No steps or box to stand on, but she straddled a corner, balancing on the narrow shelf that ran along the wall. There was nothing taped to the lightshade. She went back to the front door where a glass globe enclosed a bulb. She unscrewed the globe, and there was the key.

It fitted the back door. Half an hour to go. She locked the door behind her and slipped into the flat. The curtains were already drawn. She took a small torch from her pocket and started her search.

She found them within seconds, the only contents of the bottom drawer of the desk his computer stood on. A tidy bundle in a folder labelled CORRESPONDENCE. Freddie had given her a list of dates on which he'd written to Bradley. She checked them against the bundle. The bottom letter was the first one, the top the last. She had them all. She closed the drawer, locked the back door and went round to return the key to its hiding place. Back at the porch, she checked the street carefully before reaching high to fit the bulb in again.

The sudden blaze of light dazzled her. She moved away from the porch and stood against the wall for a moment or two while her eyes adjusted to the dark. God, if anyone came down the street and saw her now. But she had to wait; if she went blundering into things Joseph Bradley's neighbours could well come out to investigate.

The moonlight and the street lamp helped. She didn't have to wait long before it was safe to start along the path to the drive.

As she passed the neighbours' door it opened and a man came out carrying a milk bottle. She went cold. She stood stock still, maybe he wouldn't notice her. But he did. He turned, gasped, said angrily, "Who the hell's that?" It was the guy from across the road – the one who'd seen her already. Her head spun.

She swallowed. Best means of defence is attack. "Hell, you scared me," she said angrily – her voice sounded odd, echoing in her head, if he noticed he'd just think it was the fright. "Shooting out of the door like that!"

"Yeah, well... Just putting the bottle out, eh. Hey –" God, he'd recognised her! "You were in that car before. Said this wasn't the right address." He peered into the street, looking for the car.

"It wasn't," she said. "Not my starting address." Her story sprang fully fledged into her mind; she hadn't even known what she was going to say. "I had to start a way back down the other street."

"Start what?"

"Survey," she said, waving the folder of letters at him. "This was my last address, not my first one. They're fussy that you get things in the right order. I've just tried your neighbours, but there's no one home."

"Well." His teeth gleamed in the moonlight as he grinned happily. "*I'm* home. Just let me put this bottle out and I'll be right with you. You can survey me, eh. Over a cup of coffee, maybe. Or," he added hopefully, "a nightcap. Seeing this is your last address."

She forced her voice to relax, her mouth to smile. "I don't think so," she said. "The survey's for women only." Christ! She should have said for the over-sixties or something. What if he had a partner? No – he was too keen to get her inside, had tried to chat her up when she was in the car; there wouldn't be a woman there.

"That's a pity," he said. "But what about a cuppa anyway?"

"Thank you. No. I must be getting back."

"To the hubby?"

She didn't bother to answer, just moved past him.

"Where's your car?"

"Around the corner." She was nearly at the drive by now. The bastard was hulking along beside her.

"I'll walk you down to it. Not always safe on the streets, eh, once it's dark."

God, what if he jumped her? She'd done self-defence; it wasn't *that* that she was worried about, big and all as he was. It was a vision of the letters scattered all over the place. She gripped the folder more tightly. "I'm perfectly safe," she said coldly.

"Oh, don't worry," he said, changing her meaning, "so'm I. I'm with the police."

The police! He was joking, please God let him be joking. She looked sideways at him as they walked. He nodded, friendly, non-threatening. "Detective Senior Sergeant Rangi Roberts," he said. "At your service, ma'am."

He wasn't joking. Hell and shit and bloody damnation. There was nothing for it. She suffered his presence beside her as they walked. "And you are?" he asked.

"Joan Williams," she said, giving the name she'd used when she'd hired the car.

"Mrs? Miss? Ms?"

She didn't reply.

"Well, here we are," he said as they reached the car.

"Yes." She unlocked the door. "Thank you."

"A pleasure. A real pleasure... I hope I see you round."

She turned the folder of letters over so he wouldn't see its title, leant over and shoved them into her open satchel on the passenger seat.

"No clipboard?" he asked.

"Pardon?"

"Survey people always seem to have clipboards."

"...I forgot to bring it."

"Ah."

She got in, put the key in the ignition. "Well," she said. "Thanks again."

"No problem. You live round here?"

"No," she said shortly, and started the engine.

She was just pulling away when he tapped her window. She longed just to drive off, but... but he was a policeman. She stopped and let the window down.

"Just wanted to check. That's a rental car, eh. Or you're not used to driving it."

Christ! How did he know that? Her heart thudded. "What makes you think that?"

"This afternoon, when I saw you, you pressed the wrong button and the window went up instead of down."

"The window went up," she said, amazed at how cool her voice sounded, "because I didn't want to speak to you. I know perfectly well how to work it. See?" She pressed the button and the window slid silently, firmly, shut.

As he walked back to the flat, Rangi swore at himself. He was always doing that – coming on too strong when he liked the look of someone. It scared them off. They backed away like he backed away when women suddenly threw themselves at *him*. The trouble was, it was always the wrong women who did that, ones that simply didn't turn him on. Now if that one had been keen, it would have been a different story. No backing off then.

Oh well. He opened the door. Another bloody evening of tv. He put the kettle on. Wisps of long fair hair peeking out from under that dark beret – real style, she had. Unrelieved black clothing looked stupid on some women, not her. Good car, too. *Not* a rental; so much for you, Holmes. *The window went up because I didn't want to speak to you.* Elegant, cool. More than cool... cold? Those gloves, and the evenings were pretty warm already. Pity about the gloves though, he could've checked to see if there was a wedding ring.

Forget it, he told himself. She's way out of your field.

Must be difficult to take notes in a survey with gloves on. Especially when she'd forgotten to bring a clipboard. Standing there in doorways, interviewing, balancing a stack of papers... Shit, forget her. Probably married with a raft of kids and doing this to eke out the family finances. Using her husband's car in the evenings.

She didn't *look* married.

Not married with kids, anyway.

Probably a business executive just made redundant. He searched through the litter on the bench for the pack of tea bags.

Julia couldn't drop the car off straight away. That afternoon she'd rushed into the rental firm with a story about her car breaking down. She had to attend a meeting out of town. She didn't have her licence with her, was just visiting from Auckland, but would her bankcard be ID enough? (Her bankcard gave her name as simply J B Williams.) She'd be doing around fifty kilometres and would drop the car off when she got back later that night. Could she pay in advance?

She could. They took down the fictitious details of an Auckland address and phone number, accepted cash and showed her where to drop the keys when she returned the car.

So now she had to drive twenty-five kilometres out of town, and twenty-five kilometres back so they wouldn't think it odd when they checked the milage. Then she'd have to collect her own car and do the long trip back to Auckland.

All she wanted to do was crawl into bed, pull the covers over her head and forget the whole wretched business. She'd really stuffed up. How would she be able to tell Freddie? He was flying back up to Auckland in the morning, and then on to Australia. She was to meet him at the airport.

Freddie. Part of her resented the weakness he'd confessed to her. His lapse, even though it had brought them closer, had left something sour in the way she felt about him. She didn't like to think of him as having any frailties, but of course he did. And it was his imperfection, after all, which had enabled her to offer him such a proof of loyalty that...

Yes, well, it hadn't worked out, had it? A bloody *policeman*!

That was twenty-seven kilometres. She slowed, swung the car round and headed back to town. A disaster of an evening.

Joseph Bradley was having a wonderful evening. Frederick (they were on first name terms straight away, of course) understood his work so well. Frederick listened entranced as Joseph described his writing methods, outlined the plots of possible future novels. "I have just so many things that are waiting to be written," Joseph said.

Frederick nodded. "I know what that's like," he said. Frederick took Joseph seriously.

The only thing that marred their time together was that there was no one to see the two of them chatting away like the firm friends they were so rapidly becoming. Frederick had invited Joseph to his hotel and had had a meal sent up to his suite. "So that we can talk without interruption."

In any case, the whole world would know soon enough that Joseph and Frederick were intimates. They'd know, too, what talent there was in the man they had despised and plotted against. Fools. It took someone of the calibre of Frederick Tapper to understand the subtleties of Joseph's mind.

Frederick obviously valued their blossoming relationship – he had ordered champagne, though he himself drank only iced water. Which showed how little those people knew who hinted that Frederick might have a drinking problem – there had been an snide article in a recent publication. The man was abstemious, an ascetic, like Joseph. Though Joseph, of course, did indulge a little in the champagne; it would have been rude not to, and it was a vintage after all.

In fact, by the time the evening drew to a close and Frederick, looking at his watch exclaimed about the time, Joseph had nearly finished the whole bottle. He was still perfectly in control, naturally. "I'm off on a tour of the States in a week or so," Frederick said, "so it'll be more than two months before I get a chance to write to you again. Don't think I've forgotten you just because you don't get any letters for a while. Keep sending anything you want me to see and I'll get to it as soon as I'm back."

Of course Joseph understood. A tour of the States – *he'd* be doing tours like that soon enough. Frederick yawned. "I'm booked on an early flight tomorrow," he said, "so I'd better hit the sack now. It's been great meeting you, Joseph. I'll see you to the lift."

"No, Frederick, don't trouble. You need to get your rest. I can find my own way out perfectly well."

They shook hands. A warm, firm handclasp. Frederick patted Joseph's shoulder, and they parted. The Jaguar floated away down the street to the small flat, while Joseph hummed tunefully, happily.

He would not go to bed straight away; he would sit up and re-read every one of Frederick's letters, re-live the burgeoning friendship that had been so warmly cemented by their meeting. Their historic meeting.

But when he got out of the Jaguar he lurched unexpectedly and hit his head on the wall of the carport. The path, as he made his way along it, was strangely unsteady, jiggling insanely in the moonlight. He felt queasy – more than queasy. He only just had time once he'd got the back door unlocked to rush into the bathroom where he was disastrously ill. When it was over, he staggered off to bed, thankful to the depths of his being that Frederick had not witnessed his disgrace.

And that was why, for the first time since he'd moved in, he did not check before opening the back door that the small thread of black cotton which he always inserted as he locked it, was still in position. It was a precaution he had begun to take years ago when he first suspected that he was being watched. If the thread were not in place, he would know that They had managed to gain access and that They were in all probability waiting for him inside.

The next morning, his head still raw and his stomach still very touchy, he winced as he bent to pick up the thread from the floor and place it on the kitchen window-sill. Dear me, he had been very under the weather – and it had hit him so quickly! It was a good thing that They hadn't chosen last night to make a move, he'd never have known They were inside! In fact, though his time with Frederick – every moment of it – was clear in his mind, he had only the vaguest flashes of memory of getting home and getting into bed.

Julia and Freddie had breakfast at the airport. He'd already gone through the ticket and passport bit by the time she arrived. "I told Bradley I was going on tour for a while," he said. "So he won't be expecting any more letters. God, it was the most excruciatingly boring night of my life!" They carried their trays to a table. "How was yours?"

She didn't beat about the bush, she told him straight away, ashamed, not able to look him in the face.

When she'd finished he just sat there. After a while he said, "So?"

"Darling Freddie, what do you mean, 'So'? The bastard was a policeman – a *policeman* – and he saw me. He was suspicious too – where was my clipboard? Was the car a rental? He'll remember me all right, they're trained to remember. If we went ahead... if anything happened to Bradley, he'd be on to me like a shot."

"You got the letters, though?"

She opened her satchel. "Do you want them?"

"Might as well." He transferred the folder to his own brief-case. "Now look," he said. "We've already planned this whole thing. You've got loads of time to pick out a good place for it to happen. No one apart from hotel staff saw him arrive last night, and they have to deal with hundreds of people each week. There's nothing now to connect us with him apart from what happened last night."

"And isn't that enough?"

"No." He smiled at her warmly and his hand covered hers for a brief moment. "No, my dear. You're as paranoid as he is. Use your head, woman. It won't happen for a couple of weeks. You'll be driving your own car, not that rental. The fact that he is the victim of a hit and run accident down there and that later that night you have a puncture and run into a lamp-post up here... well, what on earth *is* there to connect you? Shit, this policeman was obviously smitten – perfectly understandable, too – and simply using whatever means he could to get you to stop and talk. You can't in all seriousness think he'll connect the luscious dish he tried to chat up nearly three weeks ago with the fact that his nasty neighbour's been killed by a car, probably driven by drunken hoons?"

Frederick watched her carefully. It had been hard enough to agree to it, but he was buggered if he wasn't going to make her go through with it now. Whatever happened to her, he was clear. If she got done for it, he could quite simply deny that there'd been any collusion. He had the letters... If she did get done for it, for that matter, she'd be mad to implicate him. The worst that could happen to her would be a manslaughter charge; bring Frederick's name into it, and their motive, and it would be seen to be murder. With a squirm of the stomach he remembered her face when she'd threatened him. *He'd be likely to tell the world if he knew you'd been holding his books back from publishing.* If the bitch thought she could blackmail Frederick Tapper and then have him all sympathetic and understanding when things went wrong, then she had another think coming.

He put his hand over hers again, left it there, rubbed his thumb over her fingers. She looked at him now with big pooch eyes. "Believe me, Julia. I understand the stress that you're under, and I do realise what you are prepared to do for me. I am grateful, you'll find me very grateful."

Christ, the eyes brimmed over! "Oh, Freddie," she whispered. "Freddie!"

And then, thank God, his flight was called. He let her cling to him as they parted, returned her kiss with a warmth he knew she looked on as a promise. "Keep in touch," he said.

FIVE

It was several days before Joseph discovered that the letters had gone. He had not, of course, heard from Frederick who he imagined was by now addressing some prestigious American group. And it seemed that the receiving of a letter was something that Joseph had come to look forward to almost in the same way a smoker looks forward to the next cigarette. A treat in store. Was it time for another one yet?

It was a Saturday morning, Joseph had done his weekend chores around the place and went out to check his mail box before settling down to a weekend's writing. The empty box produced a pang of unease. Perhaps, deep down, there lurked the hope that Frederick – his friend – might take time out from his busy schedule to drop him a postcard.

He decided to write to Frederick before getting to work. First, though, he'd go through Frederick's letters... and the drawer was empty.

For a while he sat there, the blood loud in his head. He knew what had happened. It was Them. They had broken in somehow, sometime. They had not realised that naturally Joseph would not be fool enough to keep hard copies of what he had written about Them. The folder of Frederick's letters was labelled simply CORRESPONDENCE; They must have thought that They had what They came for. Evidence that They could take to the police, or that They could use for blackmail.

Uppermost in his mind was a desolate feeling of loss and a sick anger that his place – his very private place – had been violated. Those letters were among his most valued possessions and they'd been taken by criminal thugs who... by God, he'd get back at Them! They would suffer!

Had They checked his files? Had They somehow discovered his protection codes? He switched his computer on, called up the file They would have been looking for. If anyone had attempted to break into it, the programme would let him know. It seemed normal – all entries were still there.

But if They could get into his flat without leaving any sign of Their entry, They would also perhaps know what codes he used. If They had powerful binoculars and were the other side of the street...? But he had positioned the computer so that it could not be seen from the windows.

If They had got into his house to take the letters, They could have got in earlier – before they got in this time, long before perhaps. Perhaps even before he moved in. They could have set cameras... Joseph Bradley got up and spent a long time going over every section of the wall, the ceiling, the floor, the furniture. He could not for the life of him tell where a camera had been hidden. They were dangerously clever. But a camera must be there somewhere. How else would They be able to get into his protected files and not leave a trace of Their being there?

He had known that his every move was watched, but he had not realised that he had been watched so closely. The heat in his head had now subsided. Now he was icy cold and thinking clearly.

They had got in without leaving any sign? Simple. They had obtained a key from the estate agent. Maybe one of Them even worked for the agency. And if They were watching him closely They would know about the black thread he put in the door – They would simply have replaced it as They left.

He wondered again about the fact that he had found himself living next door to a policeman. Had the police been aware of his activities even before he shifted to the flat? Was it the big Maori who was watching – a closed video circuit that simply fed through to next door? Joseph was near to vomiting.

But why take the letters from Frederick if They knew how to get into his files, to get at the letters, the evidence, They really wanted? That didn't make sense... Yes it did. They wanted Joseph to *know* that They had been there. They had wanted to hurt him, and They had chosen the very thing that would hurt him most. Dear God in heaven, They knew as much about him as that!

He felt dirty, besmirched, invaded.

He went into the kitchen and with trembling hands made himself a cup of tea while he waited for the pulsing in his head to settle again. When it had eased, he considered what his next move should be. What *Their* next move would be likely to be.

If the lout next door was not involved already, would They go to the police with Their evidence? That was highly probable. He put his cup on the bench and went back to the computer to wipe the entire file of anonymous letters. At the last moment, he reconsidered. He *liked* these letters, was proud of his turn of phrase. He copied them onto a disk before wiping the file. They might see him doing it, but They wouldn't know where he hid the disk.

There were, however, computer experts who could recover things that you had wiped by accident. Or on purpose. If the police were called in, they would know such things, would be able to call up the erased file. The only way he could be safe was to destroy the whole computer.

His novels were on computer. Frederick had the only hard copies in existence. Joseph opened a new pack of floppy disks and copied all his work, all his records. He was aware now that They were watching or that the hidden camera was recording his every move, but there was nothing he could do about that.

He would take the disks to work with him, find a suitable hiding place. Perhaps he could just keep posting them to himself. He wouldn't put them back on computer – he thought of Them reading his work, Their coarse lack of understanding of the subtleties of his writing...

He copied lecture notes as well so that they could be transferred to the new computer. When the copying was finished, he unplugged the machine, opened the battery compartment and removed the battery. He would have to move quickly – if They were watching him "live" then They would see what he was up to and get the police in straight away.

He unscrewed the computer cover and with the screwdriver gouged deep lines across the boards. Then he disconnected the monitor and took it into the kitchen out of harm's way, fetched a bottle of methylated spirits from the medicine cupboard, sprinkled it inside the computer case and set fire to it, standing by with a cushion in case the flames got out of hand.

The stench was atrocious, but he looked up through the acrid smoke and grinned. "Now, try to prove anything," he said to the air around him. He had Them beaten.

When it was over, he put the stinking remains in a carton and took it to the refuse recycling plant. He had to pay five dollars for the privilege of dumping it!

He visited the computer dealers and found to his delight that a model just like his other one was available then and there.

He was too het up to eat, but made himself another cup of tea and took two aspirin while he thought long and calmly about what Their next move would be now.

They had his letters; They knew how valuable these were to him. And the letters were all They had.

Unless, of course, They had copied the file of the other letters.

But if They had, then They would be hard put to it to prove that he was the writer.

So, They would decide to use Frederick's letters – They would hold them to ransom perhaps. Hostages for his "good" behaviour. *You will cease your investigations into the peccadillos of those around you, or we will destroy the whole correspondence between you and Frederick Tapper.* They were low enough for that. They hated him, despised him, and must resent his knowledge of Them as much as he resented Their pillaging his property.

He waited on tenterhooks for nearly a week. He couldn't concentrate on his work; his lectures droned away into incoherence. Students complained to the Dean, who had Joseph in for a very unpleasant, stupid, interview. As soon as he got home that afternoon he worked with a blanked out screen while he hunched over the keyboard and typed a short note to the Vice Chancellor about the Dean's drinking problem. He held a towel over the printer as it ran off a copy and printed an envelope so that the camera would not be able to record it. It was the first such note he had written since Their invasion, and even though he couldn't save the text, he felt better for having done it.

But he still couldn't settle down to write. When were They going to make contact? If he was right about Their using Frederick's letters to get at him – and of course he was right – They would surely be getting in touch soon.

So when, a few days later, the phone call came, he was not surprised.

It was a woman. He did not recognise her voice. Indeed the call began with her saying that Joseph wouldn't know her. "But I'm Joan Williams..." *That* was obviously a false name – why didn't They just say Joan Smith? Joseph's head was pulsing. "I'm Frederick Tapper's agent. He has told me about your work – I hope you don't mind, he did impress on me that you are not yet ready for it to be known that you are writing. Frederick speaks very highly of you and he actually let me read a little of *The Pungent Collection*." They'd have got the title from the letters; this was Them all right. "I thought that what I read was startlingly good, and would like to meet you. Perhaps it is time you considered having a literary agent..."

By God, They were clever! Had Joseph not been aware that They had the letters, he'd have believed her.

He'd go along with it for now. Let Them think They had him fooled.

She wanted to know if by any chance he would be free that evening. As if They didn't know that he rarely went out!

"I'm calling from Auckland," she said. "I'm afraid I can't get down until fairly late, and I'm leaving the country on business tomorrow. But if you are free, and could meet me, I would be delighted."

"I do happen to be free," he said, "oddly enough." The irony was wasted on her.

"I don't know the town very well," she said. "I'll be driving down. But I have a friend who lives on the corner of Cowper and McGonnigal streets. Number forty-five. Could you possibly meet me there at, say, nine o'clock and we'll go somewhere cosy for a chat?"

Cowper and McGonnigal? A part of the notorious city council housing area commonly referred to as Poets' Corner. A highly suitable venue for the sort of thing she had in mind. "I'll wait at my friend's," she went on, "and you can collect me from there."

"Certainly," he said and added, remembering that he should be flattered at the attention of Frederick's agent, "I look forward very much to our... assignation."

"Parking is a little difficult," she said. "I usually find a place at the end of the street, though, and walk down from there."

"Very well. Number forty-five you said?"

"That's right. On the corner. You can't miss it."

"Until this evening then. Thank you for calling."

They would almost certainly be offering him Frederick's letters back. But there could possibly be an even more sinister motive for the appointment. Joseph would take precautions...

Julia wiped her hands on a tissue as she hung up. She'd done it. It was all set up now. All she had to do was stay calm. Earlier she had rented yet another car – in Auckland this time – and had spent two days cruising the streets of the small city looking for a suitable place. If only she'd been able to lure him onto a small, dark, country road. But even an unsuspecting man would wonder at a literary agent's setting up a meeting in the middle of nowhere. And this guy was the suspicious type to start with. And a prick. That thin, prissy voice – *I look forward to our assignation.*

The street she'd chosen was as good as she'd find anywhere. It was short, the top bar of a T, with parking permitted only on the side opposite number forty-five or, as she'd told him, at the north end of the street. And the footpath was a mess of old cartons, boxes of cans, rubbish bins, kids' tricycles. No one in their right mind would try to pick their way along it in the dark. If he parked at the end he'd walk along the road to the corner. If he parked opposite, he'd have to cross the road. Either way he'd be an easy target.

And the street would be empty. She'd spent two evenings parked there, watching. There were lights in all the houses, but no traffic, no people. Loud music, televisions blaring, shouting, a fight one night from the sound of it. But no one in doorways or windows. At nine o'clock on both nights those who were going out for the evening had left and no one had come back until well after eleven.

She'd get there at eight and wait at the south end of McGonigall Street some distance from the corner. There was no problem about recognising Bradley, he'd be driving his Jag. As soon as it came into sight she'd start her engine. It would be all over in less than a minute from then. She forced herself to think of what it would be like. She hadn't told Freddie, but she realised she'd have to... not only knock him down. Once he was knocked down she'd have to back over him to make sure.

Once it was over came the dangerous bit. If he was found quickly, the police might set up a blockade. But it was a risk she'd have to take. Drive like hell – no not like hell, a speeding ticket was the last thing she wanted – drive as fast as she safely could back home. Put the car in the garage, wash it thoroughly then drive out and ram whatever bits were already dented into a lamp-post somewhere. Hammer a nail into a tyre to explain the crash...

She would have to back over him to make sure...

She was trembling, which was ridiculous. She looked at her watch then picked up the phone and called Freddie. His voice was warm, reassuring... loving? "I know what you're going through, my dear," he said. "I just wish I could do it for you."

"Darling Freddie, I'm perfectly all right. Perfectly all right. It's all set, all planned. Nothing can go wrong."

But something did. Ridiculously, considering she'd had her safety belt on, Julia managed to knock herself out. Her last memory was of seeing Joseph Bradley picking his way delicately down the road, of putting her foot down hard on the accelerator. Then there was nothing. She had come to, wondering who had left the tap dripping. She could hear the steading plopping of water and she seemed to be asleep in a most uncomfortable position. She was shivering with a cold that penetrated to her very brain. Her forehead was resting on something hard. Thin and hard. She opened her eyes. She was in a car. Her car. Her head was pressed against the steering wheel. Why...? Then she remembered.

Her stomach churned and there was burning in her throat, her mouth filled with saliva. Not *now*. She swallowed fiercely and forced herself upright, opened the car door so that the interior light came on. There was blood, gleaming and sticky on one hand, on the steering wheel. Her jeans were drenched and dark with it. Not a dripping tap. Her own head. Gingerly she felt for the wound. The hair above her forehead was soaked, she probed carefully. Not much pain, not much swelling. Pull yourself together, get away, drive off.

It was freezing. How long had she...? The dashboard clock said 9.05. Only a moment then. Had she... had she done it? She must have – done it and then knocked her stupid self out. She looked at the houses. Lights, sound, but no people that she could see. No witnesses. But if there had been witnesses maybe they would be phoning the police right now. Get *away*!

Witnesses to what? Was he dead? She *had* to see – only a moment, be quick. She tried to get out of the car, but the safety belt held her back. She struggled with it – it had caught around the stem of the handbrake – that was why it had not restrained her at the moment of impact.

There had been a moment of impact. She managed to release the catch at last and stepped out of the car. Her head was throbbing now.

There was no body – Christ, she'd missed him. Or had she hit him slightly enough for him to have made off for help? Then she saw a dark shape on the road some metres ahead. Her legs trembled as she forced herself towards it. It was – had been – Joseph Bradley. There was no doubt that he was dead. God – he must have been thrown all this way. No need to back over him – no one could look like that and live. This time she swallowed in vain, her stomach heaved and she spewed, spattering the road – his legs... she heaved again and again. Get *away*!

six

The death of Joseph Bennet Bradley caused considerable local, though not national, stir. Citizens who lived on the fringes of Poets' Corner had always been loud in their complaints about the behaviour of local hoons. Police were frequent visitors to the area. Now this had happened. It was obvious that this latest outrage had been perpetrated by some drunken lout from the area. Hit and run accidents usually did not hold the public's interest for long but this one had occurred after a spate of housebreaking and petty theft in the surrounding area, and pressure was put on the city council to clean up their act and the streets. The city council put pressure on the police (on Sir, himself) to find the driver responsible.

And Sir put pressure on Rangi. The victim had been Rangi's neighbour, so Sir reckoned Rangi would have more than usual interest in bringing the criminal to justice. Get him off his backside and out of the office as well. Time he got a bit more field work in. Yeah, and so what if this sort of thing was usually the uniformed branch's job? The city fathers were after blood, and it'd look good if Sir could tell them he had a Detective Senior Sergeant on the case.

Besides, the way Rangi had been performing lately, it'd probably be good for him to get back into practice doing the routine inquiry stuff that the uniformed lot usually got landed with. Rangi could well be back there in uniform if he didn't pull something out of the bag soon; this little affair might soften the culture shock for him if, *when*, that happened. And no, Rangi could not have a full team. It was only a hit and run after all. He could have pretty Pike, the racing tycoon's son, and that was it, mate. And lab facilities, naturally.

The preliminary lab reports were already in. It hadn't been exactly a hit and run. Someone – presumably the driver of the guilty car – had bled and vomited at the scene. So it was more like a hit, get out and have a look, and run. Samples had been taken – they'd be DNA typed.

Minute flakes of red paint had been found on the body. Chemical analysis had yet to be done, but it looked as though the paint was the standard red that Toyota had been using for the last eighteen months. The likelihood was that the car had been fairly new. It would be dented – perhaps not badly, but dented sufficiently for paint to have chipped off. And from the way the body had been hit there would probably be blood and tissue flying up to adhere to the under-side of the chassis.

So all Rangi had to do was find a new, dented, red Toyata. Who the hell in Poets' Corner would be likely to be driving a new car? The next couple of days were unpleasant. Rangi and Pike traipsed from door to door. A few inhabitants of the area claimed to have heard a squealing of brakes and a loud crash followed by the tinkling of glass – well, either they were making that up (there was no broken glass anywhere near the body) or they'd heard another crash altogether.

Which was quite likely – there were skid marks and glass on the road at the intersection, but they were too far away to be connected to the fatal accident. Just coincidence. Not one of those who had heard a crash had bothered to go out to investigate. Loud noises were part of life at Poets' Corner. Rangi and Pike plodded on, inspected the contents of carports, visited garages and panel beaters. It was not that they found no dented cars. Few of the cars owned by the inhabitants of Poets' Corner boasted unscathed bodies. Most were heaps of rust with crumpled doors, bent bumpers, side panels and bonnets which sported huge craters.

No panel beater or garage reported any red car's being brought in for work on something that could have been caused by the hit and run. Rangi had Pike go through all local insurance companies' accident reports and interview the owners, but he drew a blank – as Rangi had thought he would. The car that did it would probably be well away by now, might turn up a year or so later a submerged hulk in some river, and who, by then, would be able to tell for sure that it had been the one responsible?

Rangi recognised Bradley's Jag parked at the end of Cowper Street. "Better have that moved," he said. "Wonder the locals haven't got at it already; it's not their sort of car."

There was the inquest to attend and next of kin had to be notified of course. Rangi and Pike went to the university to find who Bradley's next of kin was. A pretty, flustered clerk in the Registry sorted out his employment contract and original application forms. "Goodness!" she said. "He didn't fill the *next of kin* in. Funny that no one noticed."

"He been here long?" Rangi asked. "Where did he come from?"

"Nearly three years. He was at Victoria before this. It's got his Wellington address here, and referees' reports. Maybe they could help... I'll run you off a copy, shall I?" Her smile at Rangi was too bright, too hopeful... and she was too skinny.

"Good one," he said. Bugger.

Victoria University no longer held information about Joseph Bradley. Rangi put calls through to the two referees, but neither of them could be found. He left messages for them to call him at work.

"Better go round to his flat. There'll be something there to let us know who his relatives are."

Bradley's keys were with his personal effects. Rangi checked the other objects in the plastic bag:- wallet, driver's licence, small change, neatly folded handkerchief, pen, notebook. He flicked through the grimly stained notebook – mostly empty, some small cryptic scrawls on the first few pages. What would Holmes make of all this? *The deceased, Watson, was obviously neat to the point of fussiness. There are no photographs of loved ones, no wads of receipts or used movie tickets in the wallet – he was one who kept his affairs always in perfect order. The man was, in fact, a pernickety prick, as if we didn't know that already.* "I'll take the notebook too," Rangi said and he signed for that as well as the keys. "It might be useful."

"What about the licence, Sarge?" said Pike.

"What about it?"

"Why don't you take that? You have to put down next of kin when you apply for a licence, eh. And the traffic department won't throw their records out."

"Just what I was going to say myself. Good one, Pike, we'll make a pork of you yet." Sometimes Pike really got up your nose. Rangi took out his notebook and copied the licence number.

The traffic department had the name and address of next of kin. Bennet Bradley, 4 Marsden Place, Karori.

The licence application had been made some years before, at the time when licences no longer had to be renewed every year. The chances that Bennet Bradley still lived in Karori were remote. Telecom reported no one of that name at that address. Typical. Rangi was about to phone Wellington Central to see if they could help when he realised that 4 Marsden Place was the address Bradley had given on the application forms the skinny woman in Registry had copied for him.

And the bastard's name was Joseph Bennet Bradley. He'd given his own name as next of kin.

Well, Holmes, what do you make of that?

The deceased, Watson, was of a pathologically secretive nature. Or he had something to hide. And it is that, Watson, that leads me to deduce that this is not a simple case of hit and run, but a much more serious affair altogether.

Holmes! You can't mean...?

Yes, Watson. I am very much afraid that Joseph Bennet Bradley is the victim of a particularly cold-blooded murder.

Some bloody hope.

"Here's his car key." Rangi detached it from the others and handed it to Pike. "You better drive the Jag round to the station garage. We don't want it covered in spray paint when whoever gets his stuff comes to fetch it." Whoever gets his stuff – there'd be a will with luck; that'd help him trace the next of kin. Shit, everyone had *some* next of kin. "You can drop me off at his flat and then come round to pick me up when you've seen to the Jag."

Before going into Bradley's place, Rangi checked both letter boxes. Junk mail only in both of them. He went round to his neighbour's back door.

The flat was spotless. A computer and a telephone stood on a desk, there were drawers of papers – lecture notes – neat files of household receipts – a telephone directory and a university phone and address directory which had neat asterisks pencilled beside several names, but which was otherwise pristine. A stapled wad of photocopied sheets of names and addresses headed "Society of Authors." This, too, had a few pencilled asterisks. Local names. A pair of cotton gloves in one drawer. What a geek! There were no personal letters. Maybe in the kitchen? Bedroom? Nothing personal at all. What was this guy?

Rangi turned the computer on, looked at its menu. Amazing that so short a time ago he'd have run a mile rather than come to grips with a computer. There was a file labelled correspondence. Great.

The file was empty. It had nothing at all in it. Rangi returned to the menu – no files, apart from the one labelled "Lectures," contained anything. He looked at the contents of "Lectures." That was what they were, all right.

Someone so secretive that he listed himself as his own next of kin.

Some one who kept no records apart from the completely impersonal... Rangi remembered the notebook.

Small, cramped, exquisitely neat handwriting. It was a diary – of sorts. He read through and at the end was an expert on the times and dates of Joseph Bradley's haircuts, tax returns, dental appointments. The only puzzling entry was the very last. *45 McG & C. 9.*

45 wasn't a date. An amount owing? To be paid on the ninth? ...McG & C? Rangi looked up the phone book and reached for the phone. McGraw and Cuthbertson, Accountants, had never heard of Joseph Bradley. Nor had McGrath and Cornwallis, scrap metal dealers. Or McGill, Cox and Bailey, bathroom accessories.

There was a knock on the back door and Pike came in. "Any luck, Sarge?"

"No letters. Nothing. Not a bloody thing."

"Shoot, Sarge, what do you make of that?"

"The deceased, Pike, was of a pathologically secretive nature. Or he had something to hide. And it is that, that leads me to deduce that this is not a simple case of hit and run, but a much more serious affair altogether.

"Hey, Sarge! You don't mean...?

"Yes. I am very much afraid that Joseph Bennet Bradley is the victim of a particularly cold-blooded murder."

"Je-*sus*!"

Rangi grinned at Pike's wide eyes and stood up. "You'd believe any bloody thing, wouldn't you, mate?" he said, and he hit his Watson an affectionate blow on the upper arm.

All the same, he thought later while he was having a quiet cuppa in the cafe, maybe it was murder. There were things that just didn't add up. Like why was Bradley in that neighbourhood at all? Not his sort of place... there wasn't a brothel or known house in the area, and Rangi could think of no other reason for someone like Bradley to go slumming.

And the car that did it – a newish Toyota. None of the inhabitants of Poets' Corner owned such a car. It could have been stolen, of course. Almost certainly was, if it *had* been driven by hoons from the area. But if it had been stolen, why hadn't anyone reported it missing?

The trouble was, of course, that Rangi *wanted* it to be murder. He was probably gnawing away at it simply because he wanted a more up-market crime. What would Holmes say? Rangi was buggered if he knew...

"What's next, Sarge?"

Rangi looked up. Pike was hovering beside him, a cup of coffee and a cream bun at the ready. Rangi nodded at him. "Siddown," he said. "I been thinking." He poured himself another cup of tea.

He took his time before putting it into words. It was a measure of how much he'd come to trust Pike that he said it at all. He knew Pike would not laugh or shoot his mouth off to all and sundry. To be on the safe side, though, he began with, "This is confidential, mind."

Pike nodded.

"Mightn't be such a joke, calling it murder, eh? I mean what's a guy like that doing there at night? And the car – it was new – not the sort of thing you find in that neighbourhood. If it was stolen someone would've reported it by now..."

"Yeah." Pike's face was lively with supposition. "You're right about that area. I've got a mate doing post grad work in English, and he says that Bradley was the most boring prick in the whole shop. Not the sort to be hanging round McGonnigal and Cowper."

"McGonnigal and...? Jeez!" Rangi took Bradley's notebook out. *45 McG & C. 9.*

"Drink up fast," he said. "You can bring your sticky bun with you. We got a call to make."

He was right! The house at the corner of Cowper and McGonnigal was number 45. They'd been here earlier, asking about cars, about anything that anyone had heard. Rangi got Pike to read over the notes he'd taken then. Mrs Marjorie Daley, widow and sickness beneficiary, living with her son, Roger, part-time barman. They had interviewed them both before, neither had noticed anything unusual. The son had been working on the night in question, the mother had been watching television. She was hard of hearing and had had the volume turned right up. She had not been one of the ones who reported hearing the other crash. Rangi remembered the interview; a close, surly couple.

This time they were received with even more suspicion. Red-rimmed eyes stared hostilely at the two policemen. "What you want now? I was trying to get a bit of sleep."

"Heavy night, then?"

"Arthritis. Kept me awake all night."

"Can we come in for a while?"

"Why?"

"Few things to ask you."

"I already told you what I was doing the night that man got run over. And I didn't see anything or hear anything, I told you that."

"Something has come to our attention since then, something which means I got to talk to you a bit more. Can we come in?"

"...No." The woman looked a bit scared as though she was doing something that she'd been dared to do. "No you can't come in. I told you, I'm having a lie down and I got nothing more to say. You come here, harassing me, I got rights. I can make a complaint. To my MP..."

"You want to stay out here and talk then? Or you want to come down to the station and talk there?"

Her eyes flickered to the street. Rangi turned to see what had distracted her. A woman pushing a pram was moving slowly by, her eyes glued to the trio on the doorstep. And a curtain across the road was twitched back into place.

"Not harassing, Mrs Daley. Just a few things we need to know. You can complain to your MP – or to the neighbours – if you like, but someone's been killed and it's my job to find out about it. You wouldn't want to hinder the police in the execution of their duty, would you, eh?"

She sighed exaggeratedly and turned away from them leaving the door open. Rangi took it as an invitation and followed her inside.

The door led directly into a scrupulously neat kitchen that smelt faintly of lemon and ammonia with an overlay of stale cigarettes. She pulled out a chair from beside a kitchen table and sat down carefully, grimacing with pain.

"Mind if we sit down?"

She shrugged and pulled a packet of tobacco from the pocket of her pants. With bent, lumpy fingers she slowly worked a cigarette paper out of a folder and began to arrange shreds of tobacco on it. She kept her head down, concentrating on her task as Rangi and Pike took the other two chairs at the table. Pike got out his notebook.

"That night," Rangi said, "the night Mr Bradley was killed, he had an appointment at this address. Would you like to tell us about that?"

She stopped fiddling with the tobacco. Her head came up, her eyes open wide enough to show the red of the bottom lids. "An appointment here? Like hell he had an appointment here! What you trying to pin on me? I told you I never seen him."

"Not trying to 'pin' anything on you. Just, we know he was coming here, and –"

"He was not coming here! What the hell would he be coming here for? Never seen him, never heard of him in me life before."

"What about your son?"

"Roger was working that night. He told you that." Her head was down again, she painstakingly rolled the paper up and licked the gummed edge.

"Where is he now?"

She pulled a box of matches from her pocket. "How should I know? He doesn't have to tell me where he's at every minute of the day. He's a grown man."

"You expecting him back for tea?"

"Maybe he'll turn up. Maybe he won't. No skin off my nose." She lit the cigarette and glared at them through the smoke.

"I'll need to talk to him as soon as he gets back. You on the phone?"

"You do not bloody need to talk to him. You talked to him already. He was working that night and why would he make a date to see someone here if he was working? And it sure as hell wasn't me that made any 'appointment.' My days of appointments are long gone." She wheezed and chuckled and wheezed and coughed.

Pike smiled politely and waited till the spasm was over, Rangi just waited. When he reckoned she could talk again, he asked, "Your son, he know in advance what hours he's likely to work?"

She looked at him with narrowed eyes. "Sometimes he knows. Mostly he knows. Sometimes they call him in at short notice if someone goes sick."

"That night? Was he called in sudden?"

"No."

"You sure?"

"That night was one of his regular nights. He'd of known about that two weeks in advance."

"Yeah?"

"I don't know what you're trying to prove, but you're barking up the wrong tree if you try to pin something on Rog. Doesn't even have a car." She grasped the sides of the table and hauled herself to her feet. Then she crossed the kitchen to pull a calendar down from its place on a nail hammered into the back door. "What night was it again?"

"Fifteenth. Tuesday this week."

"There you are then." A knobbly bent finger stabbed at the date. "4.30 to 12.00. He writes the times in when the schedule comes out." She slapped the calendar down in front of him. "Go and ask them at the pub, if you don't believe me."

Rangi looked at the pencilled scrawl. Several days had similar notations. Easy enough to write them in afterwards, but. "Yeah," he said. "Yeah, we'll do that. Check with the pub." He stood up. "Thanks for your help, Mrs Daley. Sorry to disturb you."

She grunted.

The hotel manager confirmed that Roger Daley had worked that night. No, there was no chance that he could have slipped away for even a few minutes around nine. The bar had been busy. A visiting band from Auckland had packed the customers in and Daley would have been missed on the instant if he'd disappeared.

Back in the car, Rangi glared at the small notebook. "What else can it be, though?" he said to Pike. "This guy's written down the address of a place that he gets killed nearly outside of, and the time – just about – when he gets killed. Why the hell would he do that unless he was bloody well going there? And if he's set up a meeting there, what the hell for? It wasn't with the son, so it must of been with the mother."

"Sex?" Pike grinned.

"Don't make me laugh." What would Holmes reckon? A well-to-do prick visiting that house... Blackmail? The old lady's a fence? He's her long lost son – just found out through adoption tracing? Nah – from what Rangi knew of the guy, if it turned out his mum was living at that address, he'd run a mile in the opposite direction. He was a snob if ever Rangi met one. He still remembered the snide "where you come from" of their first conversation – about the rubbish tin.

Yeah. *The answer is simple, Watson. The deceased, discovering to his horror, that his natural mother is an unpleasant old biddy without a penny to her name, runs desperately out into the night – and into the path of a near-new red Toyota.*

Holmes – you don't mean...?

Yes, Watson, I very much fear that the death of Joseph Bradley was nothing more than a common hit and run accident.

It wasn't impossible... Yes, it was. If that one had been his mother and he'd been killed she'd have been in boots and all for her cut of his leavings.

Why *was* he going there, then? Fence, blackmail, something to sell... what would she have to sell that Joseph Bradley could possibly want? Nothing. Rangi was willing to bet there was nothing in that

71

house that Bradley would be attracted to, that he'd touch with a barge pole. What else did people sell? Information? Yeah, maybe she knew something about someone that Bradley wanted to do the dirty on...

There were possibilities...

He became aware that Pike was looking at him. "Well, what's up? Why we just sitting here?"

"I don't know where you're thinking of going next, Sarge."

"Neither do I, mate. Neither do I."

seven

There was another letter from Joseph Bradley. Frederick shuddered. The bastard had been dead for three days. Julia's phone call had been almost incoherent – silly bitch had hit her head or something, she said – but she was clear about one thing, Bradley was dead.

And Frederick had told Bradley that he'd be out of the country for weeks, anyway. Told him to send on anything he'd written, but this envelope was too thin for that. So why was he bothering to write a letter when he thought there wouldn't be anyone here to receive it?

Aware that he was just standing there in the kitchen staring at the bloody thing with his housekeeper's interest growing by the moment, he managed a smile and a nod and took the letter with the rest of his mail into his study. Another long screed; at least it would be the last he would have to wade through.

> *Dear Frederick,*
> *I am writing to you in some haste and considerable perturbation.*
> *I am being threatened and fear, not unreasonably, that perhaps*
> *my very life is endangered.*

Frederick felt his forehead suddenly cold. He sat down.

> *Some time ago, though I am uncertain of the exact date, my*
> *apartment was entered and your letters to me – letters which,*
> *need I say?, I hold among my greatest treasures – were stolen.*
> *I know that they were taken in error; they were not the goods*
> *the criminals had intended to steal. However, because it was*
> *obviously my correspondence that was the target of the raid,*
> *I know, if not the exact identity of the burglars, at least I have*

a list of the names of those among whom one or more must be the culprits.

Joseph's impeccable grammar was breaking down. The bugger must have been really stressed.

When I discovered my loss, I immediately took a course of action to protect myself from further such intrusions. However, despite all my precautions, I know that I am constantly under surveillance. Indeed, I have suspected as much for more than a year. This morning, They (I must use the upper case, Their threat in my life looms so large. They have even suborned the police and the real estate agent so that I was tricked into taking this apartment which is right next door to a policeman, whose main duty, I am certain, is manning the hidden tv cameras in my rooms)...

The guy had flipped!

...This morning They showed their hand. I received a telephone call from a woman purporting to be – of all people – your – literary agent.

I was not, of course, hoodwinked for a moment, but let Them think that I had no suspicions. She praised my work in such terms and with such specific references that it was clear They had read your letters to me. Obviously, then, my suspicions that it was They who had previously burgled my apartment were well founded. This woman has invited me to meet her (with the bait that she will consider acting for me, and with a great deal of flattery – how little They know me if They consider I would respond to flattery!) this evening.

Now, I am reasonably sure that it is some sort of blackmail that They are considering. Perhaps They hope to offer to hand back your correspondence in return for my ceasing certain activities, the details of which I shan't bother you with, but which I have felt necessary for the good of society. I am not the sort of man to let wickedness and often actual criminality go unmentioned.

What the fuck was he on about?

On the other hand, Frederick, They may have decided to employ more drastic methods. Lately I have taken steps to conceal my actions – the computer now is completely hidden from any cameras, They cannot see what I write. This will, obviously, (and I blame myself that I did not consider the implications of my moves) have let Them know that I am "onto" Them. They may have resolved to put an end to me.

Christ!

I am, however, not the sort of man who flinches in the face of possible personal harm. Besides, I very much want your letters returned. I am not a fool though, and am therefore taking the precaution of writing this letter. If I am threatened I can tell Them of my suspicions and that I have written to a friend so that any harm that comes to me will be speedily avenged. (I shall not, of course, mention that my friend is not actually at his address at the moment!)

If, therefore, when you return from your tour of the States, you find this letter and none other informing you that I am alive and well, will you please take the following information to the police:-

1. If I have been found dead, and the death appears to have been the result of an accident, this is not so.
2. I have deposited a packet of computer disks in a locked box which you will find under a pile of old newspapers and rags in what was a cleaning cupboard and which has not been used to my certain knowledge in all the time I have been at the University. The cupboard is situated at the end of the English Department corridor, right next to my office. When I first took up my position at the University I inspected this cupboard and suggested that it be made available for the storage of some of my books (the shelving in the small room they allotted me is hopelessly inadequate). The caretaker – a miserable specimen – objected, wishing to retain, as do all petty officials, every small item, no matter how useless, that he saw as part of his domain.

Even when, at the end of a year, I could state categorically that the cupboard had been opened by no one but myself, he was adamant in his refusal to let me use it.

The key to the box is taped to the right-hand side of the curtain rail in my office. Most of the computer disks contain copies of my novels and each is labelled with a working title, so that you will recognise them easily. I have taken the precaution of wiping them all from my computer so that They will not discover them if They raid my place again. There is one disk which holds copies of my letters to you, which I have also removed from the computer. This is labelled FT – Letters, and I would like you to have it as well as the disks of the novels. But one disk, labelled simply X, I would like you to take to the police – without examining its contents. I know I can rely on your integrity in this. The police will find there sufficient evidence to point to a possible group of criminals, some at least of whom – They may all have conspired jointly for all I know – will have been responsible for my disappearance.

If, as I expect and fervently hope, I have written to you subsequently to this letter, I trust you will forget its contents and destroy it, realising, perhaps with amusement, that the alarm was simply the result of my over-active writer's imagination.

I hope that you had a very pleasant and successful tour and that your engagements were not too demanding. I look forward with impatience to hearing from you on your return.

With my best wishes

Your friend

Joseph

Shit oh dear, what now? Frederick forced his mind to quieten, his brain to work. Most of him told himself not to worry. The cops wouldn't go delving too deeply into the affairs of the victim of a hit and run. The bloody disks could moulder there for years.

It *was* being treated as a hit and run, wasn't it? Julia said it had gone off all right. But that mumbled phone call was the only contact they'd had. He'd better ring her and see what the papers were making of it. Should have done so before.

But she wasn't there. Her answer-phone's message said that she would be away for a few days. What the hell was she doing gadding around at a time like this! Should he make the trip into the city and look up the New Zealand papers to see what they said?

What if it wasn't being considered a hit and run? Or what if there'd been a witness and Julia's car identified? She'd left home, and she'd not mentioned to him that she'd be doing so. What if she was "away" helping the police with their inquiries? If they suspected... *then* they'd go rootling through every damn thing they could find.

No, the most they could get her for would be manslaughter. Dangerous driving. And if that happened she wouldn't be fool enough to...

He could rest assured. The disks in the cleaning cupboard wouldn't be unearthed by the cops. At worst they'd consider Bradley's death criminal negligence or something. They'd have no cause to suspect murder. He wondered what she'd tell the police, if she had been caught, about why she was in the area at the time? She'd have had a story ready though, surely, just in case. Julia was always prepared for any eventuality.

The trouble was, he hadn't wanted to know the details, had wanted to distance himself, stay lily-white. Now he wished he'd asked her more.

The disks. Sooner or later – in a matter of years, maybe, they'd be found.

So what?

...So they'd be found at a fucking *university*, that was what. Found at the one place that might be alerted to the similarity, the *identity*, between the books on file and those which were currently appearing under Frederick Tapper's name. Or which would be about to appear, depending on when the things were found.

But it'd most likely be cleaning staff who'd find them. Cleaning staff wouldn't suss out what they were about... Bloody hell, cleaning staff wouldn't *know* they were computer disks. Cleaning staff would find a locked box. They'd hand it in. It'd be opened, examined. Hell.

Maybe, though, it'd be a bent cleaner who found them. A bent cleaner would force the thing open, hoping to find a stash – cannabis, notes. Then what'd they do? When they discovered only computer disks, they'd get rid of the evidence of their pilfering, that's what they'd do.

It was the most Frederick could hope for.

...It wasn't much.

The door opened. "Not *now!*" his voice was startlingly loud. He swallowed, tried for control. "I'm thinking."

But the bloody woman just stood there. Frederick lifted his head to scowl. It wasn't the housekeeper; it was Julia.

Julia caught the full force of Freddie's glare and her stomach twisted with excitement. It was the old Freddie, the one she worshipped, the one who was always in control. She could forget the miserable wreck she'd had to carry to bed – that was just the drink, this was the real Freddie... With the added difference, that he owed her. *You'll find me really grateful.*

"Hi," she said and walked towards him as he slowly stood up. "Thought I'd surprise you." She put her hands on his shoulders and lifted her face for his kiss, loving the remembered scent of his aftershave.

So the police hadn't got her. He kissed her cheek, and her arms went round his neck. She wanted more. Well, she'd better have more, Frederick supposed. He turned his lips to hers and pressed down. God, she was an open-mouther! But he put his arms around her and acted as though he liked it. When she came up for air her eyes were wide and doting. Any moment now she'd put her tongue out and start a panting grin. She pressed her cheek to his – pressed everything she'd got against him – and whispered, "It's over. I did it." Shit, she was licking his ear! Frederick felt goose bumps flicker down his back.

He took her arm and guided her to a chair. "Business before pleasure," he said as he went to close the door. "You must tell me all about it. My poor love, you must have been through hell." He affected not to see her hand patting the arm of her chair in invitation for him to sit close, and moved behind his desk. "And I've got something to show you afterwards." He was beginning to see a solution to the problem of the disks. He sat down, leaned over the desk towards her, let his voice burr with symmpathy. "Was it dreadful?"

"I don't know."

"You don't *know*?"

"Afterwards was dreadful. I puked. All over... But doing it – I don't remember. I told you on the phone, I hit my head." She pushed her hair back from her forehead and gazed at him with limpid eyes. See my devotion, master; I did this for you. There was something nasty on the hairline. She – she was expecting him to kiss it better!

Reluctantly he stood up again. "Poor darling," he said, and he moved to brush the swollen red line with his lips, steeling his face to remain compassionate. At least the scar didn't kiss back.

As her arms came up to him, he put them gently aside. "Has it been in the newspapers?"

"Yes. The evening after and the next morning. I haven't seen anything since."

"Hit and run?"

"Yes, of course. I brought you a clipping." She bent down for the handbag she had put beside the chair.

"No, don't bother. I'll look at it later." He withdrew behind his desk again. "Tell me," he said. "You'll need to talk about it."

So she told him. Every little detail. Coming round, her head, the safety belt, the body, being sick, driving back to Auckland still half in a daze, washing the car. "Though I couldn't see *any* blood – it was weird. Must've been raining on the way, though I don't remember."

"I thought you said there was blood everywhere."

"*Inside* the car, Freddie. My blood from where I banged my head. But none on the outside that I could see."

"Was there blood around the – around him?"

She shuddered and nodded. "I can't remember it raining," she said again. "I just can't remember."

"You were still groggy."

"Not so groggy I didn't realise I shouldn't do anything about the bump on my head. Once I'd cleaned the car I drove to the corner of my street. I hammered a spike into the tyre before I ran it into a post at the end of the road. In case someone came straight away when they heard the crash. I thought of that just then – so I can't have been too muddled. I drove into the post and hit right on the place that I must've – on the passenger side... the bit that was smashed in already. Then I pulled at –" Her hand went to her head. "So that it started bleeding again. So it'd seem I'd done it just then." She grinned proudly.

He actually said, "Good girl." And resisted the temptation to add,

79

"Give."

"The crash made a hell of a noise. The house at the corner lit up and the couple who live there – she's Nancy something – works at a solicitor's in town – they came out. I just sat there with my head on the steering wheel like I had been when I came round the first time... They did all the right things, turned off the ignition, put a blanket round me – I let them think I'd been knocked out for a bit – called an ambulance. The ambulance called the police and I said all I remembered was a bang and then losing control of the car. The cops saw the flat tyre and that was that. The ambulance woman cleaned up my head and said I ought to have X-rays, but I went all stubborn. You know, how people do after a shock, and said I just wanted to get to bed. In the end they took me home and said I should see my doctor in the morning. Then I rang you."

"So you did." He smiled at her.

"So now," she stood up and came close, "now Frederick Tapper writes again." Her arm pulled his head towards her hip, her fingers ran through the hair at the nape of his neck. She was ready for her reward... and she was expecting something more than just a chew-bar.

"No," he sighed. "No, my dear. Frederick Tapper may never write again."

He felt her stiffen. "Freddie? But –"

He reached for Bradley's letter. "You'd better read this," he said.

She took it, returned to her chair, read in silence. Finally she raised her head. "He was mad," she said. "Do you believe all this stuff about Them?"

"Paranoid. We knew that. And your taking the letters must have pushed him over the edge. But that's not the point. Sooner or later those disks will be found. I wasn't worried about the novels' being in his computer memory – he told me a long time ago how he hedged his work around with all sorts of passwords and things. But this – " He pointed to the letter "– this means that I'll never be safe if I do... do use his work. I'd be sitting on a time bomb." He gave a brave smile. "All our work, my love, has been for nothing." He let his shoulders droop, his head sink.

She didn't point out that the work had hardly been equally shared. In one graceful movement she was out of her chair and kneeling beside him. He stroked her hair, shook his head. "It's no use," he said. "I'll just have to hope that this dry time does finish."

She wasn't having that. She nuzzled into his thigh. "Let's forget it," she said. "We'll just take the risk."

The hand hardened, pushed her head away. The wound throbbed suddenly under the pressure, but she hid the pain. "*We?*" Freddie's laugh was bitter. "*We'll* just take the risk? Who's the one who'll be pilloried if it ever comes out?" She was too scared of what she'd see in his face to look at him. "And with my luck the way it is these days, it's fucking well bound to come out."

She looked at her fingers, fingers that had clenched around the steering wheel, and swallowed. Then she said, "What then?"

"What then? Well, all I can say is, Thank you, my dear, for your trouble, but if I were you I'd start looking round for a more lucrative client."

"*Freddie!*" Now she looked at him. He was leaning back in his chair, eyes shut, misery deep in the lines of his face. She'd lost him. Just like that. She shivered and nearly moaned.

He felt her gaze, forced his mouth into a smile – such a pitiful brave smile that her heart broke. "Sorry, sweetheart," he said. "That was callous." His eyes were still shut. "Reckon it's too early for a drink? Special occasion, after all."

She was not losing him without a fight. "No, Freddie. It's much too early for a drink, and you know it." She stood up. "Besides, there's things to talk about."

"What is there for you and me to talk about ever again?"

"Don't be ridiculous. And don't dramatise yourself. What we have to talk about, Sir, is how quickly we can have lunch, look at a proposition for a radio adaptation of *Swingle* and see how soon I can get a flight back."

His eyes opened. "You're not staying?"

"I can't. I've got to get back and collect some tapes from a cupboard, don't I?"

She hadn't lost him! The glow in his eyes, the rejuvenation of his face! He was out of his chair and pulling her to her feet. She was suddenly breathless in his arms, his mouth was on hers, open and avid, his body urgent against her. When he took his mouth away, he buried it in her neck, snuffling her skin, her hair.

She'd fallen for it. And, clever lady, she'd thought of it all for herself! Frederick poked his tongue into her ear – she was obviously into ears

– and felt her shiver. "You'll stay the night, but," he whispered.
"Of course. Of course, my darling."

Bugger.

eight

She bought a faded green overall and a pair of scuffed sandals from an op shop and used the panelbeater's courtesy car to drive down to Joseph Tapper's university early on the Saturday morning. Universities were easy to get into. Their doors, on a Saturday, were open. She just walked in, overlarge sandals slopping under laddered stockings.

The English Department was on the third floor. She went in the wrong direction to start with, Professors and Associate Professors' names on the doors. She turned and made her way back, passing a man in the corridor. He nodded cheerfully. "Morning."

"Mornin'," she said and plodded on.

Joseph Bradley's name was on the left. Only one door past that, and it had no name. No lock either. She pulled the old duster she'd brought with her out of the overall pocket, put it over the doorknob before turning it. Not that there was any chance anyone would be trying for fingerprints, but she might as well take all precautions. The door stuck and she had to shove. It opened with a clang, flying back to hit a pile of paint tins. It was the cleaning cupboard.

She looked down the corridor, but no doors opened to see what the noise had been. The cupboard was large – almost a small room, but there was no light inside and no window so she had to leave the door ajar while she shifted the huge pile of newspapers and cloths. The box was a small metal cash box. A label gummed to the top. *Joseph Bradley, Private Property*.

So easy. So simple. And it was the key to a lifelong relationship with Freddie. She wanted to dance, sing, float along the corridor. Now all she had to do was destroy the thing. And that she could do in her own time. Force the lock, bend the disks, burn them – something. Then chuck the whole thing out in the rubbish.

It was over. The night with Freddie had been wonderful. He'd admitted he was really in love with her, he certainly had been an enthusiastic lover, even if not as skilled as she would have expected. He said he'd never known such amazing sex.

Darling, darling Freddie.

It had been the consummation of her years of devotion. And yet, she thought as she piled the papers back as near as she could to the way they had been, there was still a niggling doubt. Freddie needed her – he always had needed her as an agent, of course – but he needed her immediate help to get these disks. Was there any chance that his love-making had been to persuade her...?

Worry about that later. She left the cupboard, closed the door and turned to hurry back down the corridor. As she passed Joseph Bradley's door it opened quickly and she walked straight into a tall blond young man. The metal box flew from her grasp and clattered onto the linoleum-tiled floor. "Sorry!" the young man's hand was on her arm. "You okay? Didn't expect anyone to be there." He let go and bent to retrieve the box.

"What the hell are you doing, Pike?"

She knew the man who now stood in the doorway. Oh God, it was the cop. The hunk who lived next door to Bradley. Jesus wept! What had she done?

Rangi, hearing the clanging, had followed Pike out of Joseph Bradley's office. Pike was picking something up from the floor while some frump of a cleaner watched him. She turned at the sound of his voice. Oh man, this was no frump! He saw recognition widen her eyes and at the same time realised he'd seen her before. *Bumped into* her before. It was the survey sweetie from a few months back. Doing a bit of cleaning on the side – Rangi knew the sort of thing. Families pressured as jobs disappeared. Lovely ladies forced into all sorts of part-time work to pay for food, school uniforms, lotto tickets. His eyes, well-trained, glanced at her hands. No gloves this time.

And no ring. He felt himself smiling. "My," he said, "you really make a habit of bumping into cops, eh?"

Her grin was weak – she must of had a real scare, Pike popping out of the office like that. "I do seem to, don't I?" Her hand was out, expecting Pike to return whatever he'd knocked out of her grasp, but her eyes – lovely big, brown, still scared eyes – were fixed on Rangi. He ran a hand through his hair. She's interested this time, man. This time she's not the cool madam who shut the car window in your face.

Pike was shoving something at him. Rangi frowned at him. Go away, Pike. Now she'd stopped looking at Rangi and her eyes did the impossible, widened even more, as she looked at whatever Pike was thrusting towards Rangi. Her mouth opened as if in protest. Rangi looked down. Pike was holding out a small metal box. "What's eating you, mate?" He tried to keep his tone light – didn't want her thinking he was the sort who bullied the help.

Pike turned the box round so Rangi could read the label more easily. "Hey, good one! This could have something," he said.

"It's – it's mine." Her voice was really strained now. Desperate almost. She was properly scared, too, not just shocked by being knocked into.

Well, Holmes, what's your opinion of this?

Elementary, my dear Watson. The lady is keen to retrieve the box which is, according to the label, not her property but that of the deceased. Therefore the lady knows something about the deceased – which is more than anyone else in this pile of higher learning claims to do. Therefore the lady's acquaintance is to be cultivated... as if you needed a reason.

"It doesn't seem to be yours. It seems to belong to Joseph Bradley." He took the box from Pike. "His 'private property'."

She was dead white. Hell, he hoped Pike hadn't actually hurt her, knocking into her like that. Rangi put out a protective hand, touched her shoulder. "You okay?"

She nodded, grinned weakly and a little colour seeped back into her cheeks. She was clearly trying to pull herself together. Rangi nodded kindly. "Take your time," he said. "You've had a shock." He looked sternly at Pike.

She did take her time. The shoulder under Rangi's hand stiffened then relaxed. Her head was down, thinking.

Then she raised those eyes and they smiled at Rangi. Here we go again! Man, she's wonderful! "Thanks," she said. "You're right, they're not mine. But I – I *am* responsible for them. They're Joseph Bradley's."

"I know." Rangi wanted to let his eyes do the "You're a real dish" slow wander, but he remembered in time what her reaction had been when he'd tried to chat her up before and instead kept them fixed to her upper lip. He felt his own lips curving in appreciation. "And how come you're responsible for them?"

"I am his literary agent."

Now Rangi did let his eyes move – meaningfully – over her shabby overall, to the laddered stockings underneath (nice legs) and – shit her shoes were gross!

"Yes," she said. "It was easier to pretend to be a cleaner and just come up and collect this than try to get the office staff or anyone to locate it. Joseph had told me where he'd hidden it and..."

She was frantically trying to avoid saying anything that could be proved a lie. Was this guy swallowing it? She had a story – a sort of story – ready now, but... he was a trained observer. Stay cool. Give yourself time. He'll suppose that you're embarrassed being caught out sneaking around so if you need to stop and think, *look* embarrassed. She raised her eyes to his and blinked. He'd come to some decision – already. His eyes were determined. He wasn't accepting a word she said! Her throat tightened and she couldn't speak.

"I think," the big cop said. "I think I'd like to talk to you some more. Somewhere else."

He was going to take her in! Her head went cold again. No, don't try to run – they'll catch you in seconds.

"Let's get down to the car."

"You-" Her voice was a squeak. "You want me to make a statement?"

"I want you to have coffee with me." She hardly heard the words. *Freddie*! "Pike can drop us off and pick us up later."

She was really flustered. Well, caught out in gear like that, she would be. But even the shapeless overall took on luscious curves when she was inside it. Espresso Extra was the place to take her. Cosy. Let her relax, tell what she had to – with luck Bradley would've mentioned his next of kin to her – and then get down to the real business of how to make sure he saw her again.

She'd gone white again, and again the colour was coming back. It was a really neat effect. He smiled warmly. Her colour flooded in. "My – I've got a car down the road," she said.

"Leave it. We'll pick it up later." He'd sit in the back with her while Pike drove.

She thought for a moment, then almost managed a smile. "Fine," she said, and she undid the overall. She was wearing a really cute brown frock underneath. Tight waist, short flaring skirt. Pity about the stockings and shoes, but. He shook the box. "Sounds like computer disks all right. Locked. The key might be on that ring, eh, Pike."

"No. It's taped to the curtain rail. Joseph told me once." Her voice was a very good voice when it settled down.

"Curtain rail?"

She nodded towards the office door. "In there."

Pike went in while Rangi did his reassuring grin at her some more. She coloured nicely. "I need the disks," she said, "because I had a really stupid accident with his manuscripts. One of those ridiculous things. They were on my bench and I turned the jug on, forgot it, and the next thing I knew there were flames everywhere. No serious damage – just the jug and the pile of papers."

So, why hadn't she –? Pike returned with the key. "A real weirdo, eh Sarge? Secret hidey-holes everywhere."

"He wasn't a very pleasant man." This time she really smiled – lovely, lovely. He was putting her at her ease.

"Come on." Rangi decided against taking her hand just yet. "Let's get us that coffee."

"What about –?" She was looking at the box, at the key in Rangi's hand.

"Well, I'm afraid as it's property belonging to someone who's died in an accident, it'd better stay with us for a while. Until we know who gets his things." Her smile faded. Her face was so like a disappointed child's that he longed to kiss it better. "We'll see," he relented. "We'll have a look at it over coffee and see what's there. Lead the way, Pike."

The bloody dork held open the front passenger door for her. Rangi scowled at him as she got in, but there wasn't anything he could do about it.

Ashley was amazed at the way Sarge worked. Here was this woman, obviously up to something shady – and just when they'd been toying with the idea of its being murder, too. And what does Sarge do? Threaten her? Start in heavy on what the hell is she doing snooping round disguised as a cleaner? All the obvious, pompous, Sir-like stuff? No way. He softens her up, lets her think he hasn't a suspicion in the whole world, pretends to swallow this rigmarole about her being a literary agent, and takes her out for coffee! Sooner or later she'd feel safe and probably let something drop about what she was really up to. Sarge would be onto it like a flash. He was terrific. Even little things like looking grim at Ashley when he put her into the seat next to the driver. Ashley understood why that was. If she noticed – though she hadn't seemed to – she'd think that Sarge wanted her in the back seat with him, that he was keen on her. That'd make her even more confident, more relaxed... and more likely to make a mistake.

He pulled up outside Espresso Extra. Sarge was out of the car like a shot and opening the door for her. "Have a break," he told Ashley. "You can pick us up in an hour, okay?"

"Right, Sarge." Ashley chuckled to himself as he watched them crossing the street, Sarge bending protectively to her, holding her arm through the traffic.

Rangi led her towards a table near the window, his hand still absently on her elbow which he'd taken to steer her across the road. She'd not objected when he first took it, she wasn't objecting now. He ushered her into the seat facing the window so that she'd have something to look at if he got boring. Not that Rangi intended to be boring. And he sat opposite her so he'd have something to look at too. He was aware of admiring glances from other customers. So they bloody should be admiring. Especially once those shoes were safely hidden under the table.

She said nothing until after waitress had taken their orders. Then she grinned, pushed her hair back and let it swing forward again. "Well," she said.

"Well." As good a beginning as any. "So we meet again."

"Don't we? I – I'm sorry about last time."

She'd had a chance to think properly in the car. She thought she could manage it. The policeman was obviously smitten – or else he was a superb actor. Come to think of it, he might be just that. Don't forget that he is police – and fairly high up. She had a story ready now, though. It should sound all right; in any case, she had to use it – and use it fast before he started asking questions that led in the wrong direction.

She smiled at him. "I know you told me your name that night, but I can't remember...?"

"Rangi. Rangi Roberts. And," his face screwed up with effort, "you're... no, don't tell me... Williamson. Joan Williamson." He grinned triumphantly.

God, she *had* told him her name was Joan.

"Some people's names just seem to stay with me." His grin was almost a leer.

But now she was admitting to being an agent, she'd *have* to be Julia. Panic rose again. Keep *calm*, damn you. "Nearly right," she said. "Williams, not Williamson. And Julia, not Joan."

Rangi could have sworn that she'd said Joan. "You sure?"

She bit her lip and then smiled. If she kept on smiling like this he'd be hard put to keep his hands to himself. She was so lusciouly inviting.

"Actually," she said, "I did say Joan. I remember now. I shouldn't have, but bumping into you in the dark like that – and with Joseph being so secretive about his writing – I... I just fibbed. About my name, too."

"And about doing a survey?"

She looked deliciously shame-faced.

"I picked it, you remember. No clip-board."

Her eyes were full of respect. "You're trained to notice things like that, aren't you?"

"Some of it's training, some of it's – well, just the way I am."

"Anyway, I'm really sorry. For lying."

"So. I know why you said you were doing a survey, too." Holmes would have been impressed, Rangi had worked it out in a flash. He answered the query in her eyes. "The guy was pathologically secretive, eh. Didn't want anyone to know he was writing. I bet he told you to keep it dark."

Shit! He'd come up with the very line she was going to sell him! Could he read minds, or what? Was he just playing her along? She glanced at him, so big and... powerful. The thing in Julia that loved power in men stirred. She felt herself redden. Well, there was nothing to be done, it was the only story she had so she'd have to stick to it. She glanced timidly at the handsome face opposite her. "That was it," she said. "He wanted to spring himself on the amazed world with all his wonderful work. And until then he didn't want anyone to know he'd written a word."

"He was that good?" Thank God he'd gone onto another tack.

"Not bad. Not world class, mind – not like...like Frederick Tapper, for example, but I think he was publishable." Why the hell had she brought Freddie's name into this conversation? She could have kicked herself.

Even Rangi had heard of Frederick Tapper. "Do you know him? Tapper?"

She shook her head, and then – wonder of wonders! – she put a hand over his. "I'm sorry I fibbed. I just said the first thing that came into my mind. It was actually a manuscript I was returning, not survey notes. I'd been visiting another client in the area and dropped in to see Joseph. But he was out."

Rangi turned his hand over so that their palms could touch, but she'd already withdrawn. The waitress was hovering over them with their coffee and Rangi's carrot cake.

Rangi spooned sugar into his cup and stirred it. "Sure you don't want something to eat?" He eyed the cake, gleaming and dark with thick whirls of frosting.

"Not hungry, thanks." She giggled – a tricksy naughty school-girl giggle. Delight tickled through him. "The last hour or so has really taken my appetite away."

"Not the sort of thing you do every day, then?" He put down his cup and reached for the cake.

"Not at all. But I *had* to have the copies of Joseph's work, and when I heard he was dead, this was the only way I could think of getting them."

"You heard he was dead?"

"Yes."

"How?"

"Well – it was in the papers."

"Not his name. We can't publish his name till we've located his folk."

"Oh–" Now why had she gone so pale again? "Oh, of course not. I rang the university to tell him about the jug burning them, and they said he'd been killed in a hit and run. So then I looked it up in the paper. I realised it must be him, though his name *wasn't* printed now I come to think of it."

God, what a damn fool thing to say! Would switch-board staff at a university tell a total stranger about the manner of death of a staff member? Cover it, cover it. "It was someone in the English Department who finally told me," she said. "I had a hell of a lot of trouble finding out what had happened, especially when I'd promised Joseph that I wouldn't speak about his writing so I couldn't tell them I was his agent and had a right to know. In the end I told them I was... was a lawyer."

"You're good at stories, eh."

He didn't believe her. He sat there, his mouth engulfing cake and his eyes glowing at her like a lover's. He was playing cat and mouse. Again that frisson of fear and attraction. He was so masterful. But attraction was unsafe – keep hold of the facts; he is the law and you... you are a murderer.

"I am *not* good at stories. I hate lying." Her voice was too loud, the tone too vehement. A woman reading a newspaper at a nearby table looked up for a moment with a half smile. She steadied her voice. "But I seem to have had to lie a lot lately – and all because of Joseph's stupid secrecy."

He looked with regret at the last mouthful of cake lying on his plate. Then he picked it up, adding a few crumbs with a dab of his finger, put it in his mouth and smiled at her. His smile was warm, guileless – and dangerous. The cat pretends to have lost interest so that the mouse can scamper a tiny distance away. She was breathless.

"Yeah," he said, and he licked a little frosting from a finger. "Now, something you could help me with..."

Here it came.

"Next of kin. We can't find any. We've checked his birth certificate and traced his parents – both dead. Doesn't seem to have had any siblings. Parents didn't either, so there won't be nieces or nephews. He ever mention family to you?"

He was letting her run a little way. When would he pounce? "He told me very little about his life. Complained a bit about not being appreciated at the university, but we wrote – occasionally spoke – mostly about his work."

"That's a pity. You seem to be the only person who knows anything about him at all. Seems he never talked about anything but his job to anyone at the university either. And then only if he had to. I got the feeling he wasn't all that well liked."

"I'm not surprised. I didn't like him either."

"But you were his agent."

"His work showed promise. Nothing special. But now he's dead, there's one novel I might try with a publisher."

"You can do that?"

"Being an agent doesn't necessarily stop with the death of a client." She wished that he would make his spring and get it over and done with. She couldn't think clearly any more; he was too close, too big.

"Uh huh. Now, let's open his little box, shall we? See what's there."

Rangi knew she didn't realise it, but her fingers on her coffee cup were so tense the knuckles were white. She must really want to get her hands on the disks – maybe the guy was a better writer than she'd let on. Come to think of it, he must be, otherwise why go to all that bother dressing up as a cleaner? The way she was trying to hide her anxiety made Rangi feel protective. He smiled at her warmly, reassuringly.

The big cop's face broke into a smile. Lit up. He knew she knew he was just stringing her along, and was enjoying himself. Somehow she had to get herself under control. "There'll be several disks of novels," she said. "Those are the only things I'm interested in. But it would be lovely if I *could* have them."

He unlocked the box. She was right – computer disks. She made a move to put down her cup and then thought better of it. *The lady, Watson, can't wait to get her hands on these.*
"The novels are called *The Pungent Collection, Automobiles and Knickknacks, Letters – FT, Myself When Old* (he was still working on that), *A Pearl-Grey Dress, Sawing and Dipping,* and... um... *Graphic Dreams.*"

Thank heavens she'd read them all and had a good memory. And *Letters – FT* sounded just as likely a title as the rest. He sorted the disks out, but didn't push them in her direction. "There's one left over. Just called X. What's that?"
She shrugged. "Nothing to do with his writing as far as I know."
She remembered from his letter to Freddie. X was the one Freddie was to give to the police. Well, now the police had it. Had them all. This panther of a man wasn't really going to give them to her. Oh, Freddie! But somehow the picture of Freddie was the wrong one – she kept seeing him helplessly pissed, sobbing his heart out. The animal power of the man opposite her intruded. "I really shouldn't let you have these," he said.
Smile at him. Smile and stay cool.
"If I do, there's a condition..."
Keep the smile, raise the eyebrows.
"I'd really like to take you out to dinner sometime soon."

She went bright pink. God, if they got a thing going, what fun it was going to be making her change colour like this. He wondered if making love would bring on the whites and the reds. They'd have to do it with the lights on so he could find out.

"I'd love to," she said. What else could she say?

He looked pleased – as though he hadn't necessarily expected her to agree. He really was an actor, this one. "Great! What about tonight?"

She'd have to; if she refused he'd pounce right away. Hell. And yet the feeling of constraint, of *having* to fall in with his wishes was... admit it... exciting. "I do have some people to see after this," she lied. "I was intending to visit them, finish around five or six and then drive back, maybe stop off and have a bite to eat on the way. I suppose I could stay on." She smiled at him. "I wouldn't want to be too late, though. It's been a fairly exhausting day already."

"I'll bet. Good one. What time are you seeing these friends?"

"Not friends – clients." She looked at her watch. He'd told the young policeman to pick them up in an hour, and they must have been here only about ten minutes, even if it felt like more. Better be on the safe side. "In another couple of hours," she said.

"Good. We can settle back and enjoy ourselves. Another cup?"

By the time Pike came in to pick them up they were getting on great. Rangi had learnt a load about what a literary agent does – or would have if her eyes hadn't kept putting him off listening to her words, and had progressed a fair distance in the Roberts soft-sell technique, which he reckoned he'd just about perfected. The slow dropping of hints about his athletic prowess, his far from innocent past, his tough and dangerous job – all combined with "accidental" lapses into outspoken expressions of admiration. ("Sorry – I lost the track of what I was saying. You can blame your lips for it, they're just so – sorry, hell, I'm sorry. Talking to you like that, like we've known each other for years... wish we had...")

He was unbelievable. Sitting there rabbiting on like some naive swain, pretending an ingenuousness which he *knew* she'd know was assumed. A subtle mind, a very subtle mind. Enjoying his mastery, playing games. Julia had no choice but to play along, treading warily, waiting always for his spring. It was scary; it was exhilarating. And, thank God, it was brought to a halt by the entry of the young cop – Pike.

Ashley saw the two of them there in the coffee-shop window before they saw him. You had to hand it to Sarge, he was a fast worker. They were sitting there, chatting like old friends – no, Ashley saw the tension between the two heads that leant towards each other – like lovers. She wouldn't have the slightest idea that Sarge had an ulterior motive in giving her coffee. She'd probably have let out a load without realising it.

As he opened the door, Sarge looked up, stood up. The woman did, too. Sarge looked at his watch. "You still got a bit of time," he said to her. "What say we pop round to use Mr Bradley's computer and just check out that what's on the disks really *is* what it says."

She went white. Sarge must've been giving her a pretty hard time. "If you think it's necessary," she said. "But I did tell you the titles before I even saw them, so surely –"

"Of course, of course. It's just – well, I'll maybe have to tell S – I'll have to put in my report that I let you take them, and I'll get arseholes if I let them go without checking."

She shrugged. "It won't take long?" she said. "I mean, you don't actually want to *read* them?"

"Hell no. Not that I don't enjoy a good book – I read the whole of Sherlock Holmes just a few months ago."

Her colour was back. She laughed and assumed mock surprise, "That's devotion to duty above and beyond, if ever I heard it."

"I dunno," Sarge said. "I like the way he works things out from just little details." They were at the car by now, and Sarge opened the back door for her, then settled himself beside her. "We still work much the same way, you know. At least," Sarge's voice was heavy with meaning, "I do."

She gave a small squeak and Ashley grinned as he put the key in the ignition. Sarge had been working on her all right. Ashley reckoned it was murder, and chances were the crim was right here with them.

Rangi still had Joseph Bradley's keys. The flat smelt cold and unused. Pike opened the curtains and let in some light, which improved things. "Open a window, too," Rangi told him.

He got the computer up and slid a disk in. There was only one item on the disk file. *Graphic Dreams*. He opened the file. On the screen appeared *Graphic Dreams, a Novel by Joseph Bradley*. He flipped down a couple of pages. That's what it was all right. A novel. He ejected the disk and put in another. This one was called *Myself When Young*. He felt her move behind him, her hand on the back of his chair. He leant back a little to press his shoulders into her fingers.

"That's the one he's working on," she said. "It's not finished."

The next one had no title. It just started

Dear Sir
I am taking the liberty of sending you the manuscript of a novel which I have just completed in the hopes that you...

"No title," said Rangi. "Seems to be a letter."

Her hand strayed to his shoulder. "It's a whole novel of letters," she said. "*Letters – FT* is only a working title."

"Working title?"

"Something to call them by until you know you've got the right name. That's why he won't have made a title page." Her hand was warm, there was pressure there. Slight, but pressure nonetheless. The Roberts charm must be working, eh man? He ejected that disk and ran another.

Like she'd said, they were all novels. Seven of the buggers. Imagine writing seven novels! She'd taken her hand away, but he could still feel her closeness. "Here we are, then," he said. "I better have a receipt for them, eh." He opened a desk drawer – he'd noticed blank paper there when he'd first searched the flat. "Can you write one on that. Just say 'Received, seven computer disks, property of the estate of Joseph Bradley'. I might as well have a look at X while you're doing that."

She took the paper and smiled at him. That smile! "I don't think X has got anything to do with his writing," she said. "Maybe his university work or something."

He slid the disk into the slot and looked at the file. Certainly not another novel; there were over twenty items on the file. He opened the first one and read. Shit! He opened another. Christ! Were they all like this? "Pike, have a look at this." He glanced over his shoulder. She was just folding the receipt in two. "Mind waiting a moment?" he said. "You could sit on that sofa over there." This stuff was bloody dynamite. He leant sideways so that his constable could see the screen easily.

"Bloody hell!" said Pike. "Is there much of that, Sarge?"

Rangi flicked back to show the list of files. "Only read a couple,"

95

he said, "but I reckon we'd better do a printout, eh. Know how to turn this machine on?" He studied the controls on the printer.

Within ten minutes they had hard copies of every letter on file. They'd read them from the screen as Rangi had called them up, each one as terse and nasty as the last. Hell, it *must've* been murder. The number of motives he had here was mind-boggling. To tell Sir, or not to tell? Well, of course he'd *have* to. But not for a couple of days, maybe. Do some leg-work, write some reports, then spring it on the old bastard. Let him see Rangi hadn't lost his touch after all. Come to think of it, Sir was off on a conference for the first few days of the week, so that'd be a good excuse not to get in touch. *Didn't want to bother you, Sir, until I was a bit more certain. Didn't want to upset your sipping from the fleshpots of the Capital har har, as you would say.*

"We got the day off tomorrow, eh Pike?"

"Don't mind missing it, Sarge." Pike was right on his wave-length. "Not for this."

"Excellent. What say you and me do a bit of private snooping?" Rangi looked again at the addresses at the top of each page. Where had he...? He opened a drawer, shut it, tried another. There. The university phone and address directory, and under it the list of names and addresses of the "Society of Authors". He looked at the names beside the asterisks. Handy. Here they all were – all the people named in the letters.

Something white was poking out from under some paper. The cotton gloves. Well, they made sense now.

Private snooping. Ashley felt a warm glow. Sarge really trusted him, liked him. "We could start today, eh?"

"Do a bit. But I got a date this evening I'm buggered if I'm breaking." He grinned over his shoulder at the woman as he said this.

Hell, thought Ashley, the date's with her. He's still not letting her off the hook. That's Sarge all over. Meticulous. Though Ashley reckoned it was a cert that somewhere among the people these letters were written about they'd find the owner of a smashed up red Toyota. Which meant that her story about wanting the disks because they were novels must be true. Well, they *were* novels, weren't they? But maybe Sarge knew something more, something he wasn't letting on about yet. He was a tricky one. You'd reckon there was nothing going on in that big hunky head, and then wham! Another crim in the wagon.

Sarge took the copies of the letters and returned the disk to the box while Ashley shut down the computer.

In the car on the way back she could relax a little. Whatever it was on disk X – and she didn't want to know – it had obviously done what Joseph Bradley had said it would do, and had given the police a line on a whole heap of people who could reasonably be expected to kill him.

"Where will I pick you up from?" the cop asked.

"This evening? I'll come round to your place," she said. "I know where you live."

"Oh – yeah. Good. I should be free by seven. Come over a bit after that. You can stick your car in the carport – use Bradley's side – and we can go in mine. Ah – what sort of car you got?" The question was over-casual; there was an ulterior motive there. Careful.

Rangi reckoned you could tell a lot about people from the sort of cars they chose to drive. But as soon as he'd asked, he remembered, "Oh, yeah," he said. "Come to think of it, I know what sort. I saw it, eh. Back there that night you were doing your 'survey'."

She was changing colour again. He grinned to himself, nice to have something to tease her about – like lying to the police...

"Oh, that's right," she said, "But I sold that one a while ago."

Rangi shifted his leg slightly closer. Not quite touching. Yet. "You didn't buy a red Toyota, by any chance?"

"No. My car's white – a Honda. Why a red Toyota?"

Rangi chuckled. "That's the car that did it, eh. Killed Bradley."

She'd gone utterly white again. Swallowed a couple of times before she managed to speak. "You sure?"

He chuckled again and let his leg move closer to comfort her. He wouldn't have referred to the killing so straight out like that if he'd known it would upset her. "Sure I'm sure. It was in the papers, too. We're on the lookout for a fairly new, smashed up, red Toyota."

She closed her eyes and leant back, a hand wandering to her hairline. Slowly her colour came back and she opened her eyes. "I must have missed that bit in the papers," she said. Her leg was pressing on his! The Roberts' charm was working again; it was going to be some night.

They were up by the uni now. "Just down here," she said, directing Pike. As she leant forward to do so, Rangi felt the firm thigh under

97

the stocking move against him. Pike slowed. "This one," she said. Pike stopped.

"Christ," said Rangi. "This one? I thought you said you didn't drive a red Toyota." Was she one of those pathological liars? Could she simply never tell the truth?

She looked surprised. "Is it a Toyota? I didn't know."

"Didn't know?"

"It's not mine," she said. "It's the panelbeater's."

"*Panelbeater's*?"

"Yes," she said. "My car – my white Honda – is in the panelbeaters. I had a blowout and smashed into a telephone pole a couple of nights ago." Her hand went to her hairline again, this time she pulled the hair back and showed Rangi quite a nasty scar. He moved closer in sympathy. "I knocked myself out," she said. "Neighbours found me – they were wonderful, got the ambulance."

"Police?"

"Oh yes," she said. "They turned up, the ambulance driver had to call them because there'd been an injury. But once they saw the blowout they lost interest." Her smile was wicked. "Seems policemen are only interested in you when you're being naughty."

Rangi managed to play it cool. He lifted his eyebrows slightly, dropped his eyes to the swell of her breasts. "That is so true, I'm afraid," he said. And she touched his knee – a butterfly brush of her long fingers – before getting out of the car.

"Here." Pike leant out the window. "You might be wanting this." He waved the tatty overall at her. "Goes with your stockings," he said, the cheeky little bugger. But then they all laughed.

For a while when she got back into the car, Julia just sat there. The police car had swept across the road in a circle and driven off, she'd managed to smile and wave. Now, she just sat. Got her breath back, got her senses back, got her thoughts back in order.

Then she drove until she found a motel. "A unit well away from the road," she said. "I'm needing a sleep right now, and don't want the noise of traffic." What she really needed was a place to park the car where it would not be noticed by the two most observant – and disturbing – eyes she'd ever met.

Why had he told her that Bradley had been hit by a red Toyota? If there was any evidence of what sort of car had been responsible, it would have to be evidence that pointed to a white Honda...

Once inside, she locked the door, shut the curtains and headed for the phone.

Frederick had been waiting all bloody morning. She should have got everything done and called him by ten o'clock their time, eight o'clock here. And it was already getting on for midday. When the phone did ring, he yelled into it in sheer nervousness. "What took you so fucking long?"

"Poor Freddie," she said – despite the words, her voice was high, het up. "Was it a nerve-wracking wait for you?"

"No it wasn't." He had remembered himself in time. "Not for *me* – but for you... I was so worried about you, my dear. Are you all right?"

"Freddie, I'm fine."

"And you... you got them?"

"Of course I got them. Easy as pie." She hesitated a bit and then added, "That's why I'm a while ringing. I decided to get rid of them straight away. So I bought a magnet, ran it over them. Then I prised them apart and dumped each one in a different rubbish bin on the main street."

"You took the labels off first?"

"I'm not a fool, Freddie."

"No, of course you're not, my darling. You're a brave, brave, wonderful, lovely woman. Hurry back. When will you come over?"

"Soon, Freddie, very soon."

He laughed indulgently. "Not so soon that people start talking, my dear. I am so impatient to see you, but I don't want your reputation..."

"God, Freddie, this is the end of the twentieth century. And we're both free. Where does reputation come into it?"

"Your *professional* reputation, Julia. You're my agent..."

"So? We're going to be married soon, aren't we? And there's no law against sleeping with your agent."

"Of course not – it's just. Good God, you know, Julia, I *am* old fashioned. I never realised I thought this way until just now. But, now we're about to... to link our lives this way... I find.. I actually find... What a turn-up for the books, eh? Frederick Tapper's a prude!" He used the indulgent chuckle again.

"You mean, you don't want us to fuck until we're married."

"If you must put it crudely, my sweet..."

"Bit late now, isn't it?"

"You mean – after the other night? Well, yes and no. You must realise that I have a very powerful imagination; I can manage to put the memory of that right away. We'll just pretend it never happened –"

"My imagination's obviously not as hearty as yours, Freddie." Her voice was hard rather than hurt; he'd gone too far. "I can remember that night in vivid detail."

"Well, of course, so can I really, but –"

"I can remember your telling me all sorts of things, among them that you couldn't wait until we were free to be together for always."

"And I can't, I can't – but I'll have to, won't I? Just for a little while, sweet Julia. Just until we're legal." The disks were destroyed; he had the hard copies of the books. She couldn't say anything – after all, *she'd* been the one to kill the bugger. He'd have to get another agent, which would be a pity, but soon he'd have to tell her *Go home!*

Soon, but not now. Her voice showed her tension – he didn't want to upset the applecart if she was under stress and likely to do something silly. Wait a little, wait a little.

"Until we're legal, huh?"

"Let's have a double celebration," he said. "Let's have a marriage and a launch. The launch of *The Pungent Collection.* What do you say?"

"That's a year away, Freddie. Well, six months at least. Can you wait that long?"

"If I have to, darling."

"Then," he heard her sigh, "then I guess I can too."

"Brave, wonderful, clever and understanding," he said. "I don't know what I've done to deserve you."

"Neither do I," Julia murmured as she hung up. It wasn't just the events of the morning that were churning her up. She had suddenly seen Frederick Tapper for what he was. Well, not suddenly – not really suddenly. If she was to be honest with herself, she had to admit she'd *worked* at being in love with him. To start with it was easy enough; he was successful, urbane, *powerful.* His work was superb. In the years of their relationship she'd been aware, peripherally, of flaws, weaknesses, but she'd glossed them over. She hadn't *wanted* to see feet of clay.

She leant back in her chair and settled in for a good solid think. Face it; the simple fact was that Freddie was weak, not powerful.

Weak, and with all the manipulative skills of the weak. It was his writing that had given him glamour, the illusion of power. And now that he was not writing, the shimmer that dazzled had thinned, faded so that Julia could see the real Freddie twisting, wriggling, squirming as he sought security.

She'd known it since the time she'd seen him drunk, heard the truth about *The Pungent Collection*. She'd tried to forget *that* Freddie. She'd pretended that it was he who was masterminding the hit and run, that she was his valued lieutenant carrying out her master's orders...

It hadn't worked. Or, rather, it had worked for a time – when she'd gone over there and he'd been so ardent. They *had* had a wonderful night. But Freddie, of course, was needing something from her. Even as they climaxed he'd been working toward making sure she came back to get the tapes.

And she'd gone along with it. Managed to feel – thought she really did feel – the love of a lifetime. All the time she was with him she'd stayed in her day-dream world where Freddie was God. Even this morning, she'd been playing the "Freddie directs my every move" game.

So what was the difference now?

Now? Now she'd met the real thing, hadn't she? Now she'd seen true power shining in the dark eyes of someone who could arrest, imprison her. Now she really *was* defenceless – or almost. Her only defence was her quick wit.

But Rangi, she breathed his name out loud, Rangi was every bit as sharp as she was.

And he was interested in her – not only suspicious of her, but he wanted her. She could tell. Their evening would be full of danger, it would... She wished time would rush, blur and that it was seven o'clock already.

...If she was feeling like this about her policeman, what about Freddie? Did she still want to marry him?

Of course not.

Hang on, though...

Frederick Tapper was a Very Big Name. He was rich, handsome. He was a catch – on the surface, at least. Did she want to throw that away?

Rangi – she felt her heart speed up – Rangi was a policeman. They didn't earn all that much. They didn't have the glamour or the rarity of a world-renowned writer.

And there was, be realistic, very little chance that any affair with Rangi would end in marriage. More likely – her heart was pounding now – to end in a prison sentence.

Besides, she didn't *want* to be married – not unless it was to someone... well, someone big. She'd done very well without marriage until now. Well, that was because the only one she'd wanted to marry was Freddie, and he had shown no sign of...

He was showing signs now, and the reason for that was obvious. He was using her. Blatantly. Confident that her "crush" – the right word for it, she'd been acting like a thirteen-year-old – her crush would blind her to his wiles. Right, let the bugger suffer. She could – she looked at the pile of disks on the phone table – she could make him marry her, and she bloody well would.

...If she wasn't arrested for manslaughter.

Hell, even if she was. And she probably would be. That nonsense about a red Toyota, that must have been a trap. It was her car that had killed Bradley, so if any paint was left around it would have been white. And Rangi would know the killer's car was white; he'd said it had been red to see how she reacted. How *had* she reacted? She thought back – could she have given anything away? Anything more than he knew – guessed – already?

Or maybe there *was* red paint? Maybe Bradley had brushed against some battered car as he got out of his Jag. Battered red car with flaking paint...?

Thinking this way would do no good – her head was starting to spin. Do something practical like getting the disks into safe keeping; they were her marriage lines, after all.

She drove down town, found an Office Services who copied the disks. Then she posted one set to herself by registered mail and, at the local branch of her bank, she hired a safe deposit box into which she put the other set.

Then back to the motel and bed.

She really was in need of sleep; not only had she been up well before dawn, she was nervously exhausted from juggling with the truth, and especially evading the sharp mind that set traps with such swift cunning. She'd need to be rested and have all her wits about her before the evening; whatever he found on Bradley's X disk, Rangi would still have his suspicions of her.

She pulled the counterpane from the bed. That big, beautiful, controlled body was as interested in her as the clever brain was. It was unbelievable that he should be attracted, but she was certain he was. To begin with she'd thought he was pretending, trying to lull her into making a mistake. But sitting in the back seat he hadn't bothered to hide the fact that he was physically very interested in her.

Which meant that he had no qualms about the idea of sex with a suspect. He might, she thought as she tested the pillows for softness and kicked off her shoes, he might actually enjoy the extra power he had because of her situation.

She pulled back the covers and lay down. No "might" about it. The guy was definitely into power – into enjoying his power. Despite the danger she was in, she smiled, snuggled down and closed her eyes. She'd never been with anyone who was so utterly in control. Her hand crept between her legs and she speculated about the evening for a while before drifting into sleep.

But she woke in just over an hour, none the more rested for a sleep that had been full of a dream of worms, blindly mouthing and mumbling for food.

nine

Rangi was in his office re-reading the letters, copying from the university and writers' lists the names and addresses of those named in the letters.

The letters were all unsigned, of course, and each accused someone of some wrong-doing or nastiness. They weren't blackmail, they had been written purely for the vicious enjoyment of the writing. They were sick. Quite sick enough to provide plenty of motives for murder.

Rangi copied down the final address and stretched. Now, how to tackle them? Over half of them had been written before Bradley moved from Wellington. Rangi just hoped that, if it was murder, it had been local. There was no way he and Pike could start digging around in Wellington without questions being asked. Well, he could stick to the local ones to start with – and if nothing came to light then... then he'd just have to tell Sir about his suspicions and risk Sir's ridicule. (What risk? Sir's ridicule was a bloody cert.)

Rangi winced away from the thought of it. In any case, Bradley had been away from Wellington for years – surely the murderer was local. He'd have to do the local ones first in any case.

What order? Alphabetical was probably as good as anything...

"What order will we do them in, Sarge?" Pike had been hovering while Rangi wrote. "Geography or chronological or what?"

Chromological? Every now and then Pike did this to you. The little shit was showing off his megabuck education. Rangi rubbed the back of his neck. "Chromological..." he began thoughtfully.

"I see," said Pike. "If someone got a letter three years ago he's taken a bloody long time to get round to killing the guy, eh. So you reckon we better start with the most recent ones. That it, Sarge?"

Rangi stretched again, looked up and grinned at Pike. "That's it, mate; you're learning. You can get the car out while I put them in

104

chromological order."

The latest letter was one that had been sent to Income Support. About a couple on the writers' list.

Sereyna Kirby, sickness beneficiary, is living in a de facto relationship with Simon Kerr and he supports her household.

Not the sort of thing that people might be expected to kill about, but they were first on the chromological list, and the proper way was to plod through the detail in order. Rangi grinned – at least these enquiries were going to be a sight more interesting than the last few days' plod had been.

He called Income Support, who were not parting with any information, not to anyone. If he was Police, he would know the proper channels and could avail himself of them.

Rangi swore and then remembered Shirley. They'd gone to a few things together, but she wasn't all that keen on going to bed and she'd taken to dawdling past photo shops trying to get him to say which wedding dress he liked the most so he'd lost interest. Shirley was quite high up in Welfare.

She was delighted to hear from Rangi. It'd been weeks – she'd telephoned his flat a couple of times but there was something wrong with his phone, did he know? It rang all right and she could hear him answer, but he kept saying, "Hello," as though he couldn't hear her voice. And then he'd just hang up.

"That bloody phone acting up. I'll have to get them out again."

So, when was Shirley going to see him again? Tonight? She did this little girl voice that really didn't suit someone her size.

Well, tonight was a tough one, work was really piling up at the moment – you had to work late and forget about days off, eh. Still Rangi'd reckoned he'd better give her a call to let her know he was still around, eh. Even if he was too busy for... Hey, yeah, next week was possible – he'd say distinctly possible if he could get through – Hey! He'd just had an idea – something maybe Shirley could help him with, speed things up a bit, get him a bit of spare time even, eh – slow as hell going through the proper channels with the lot she worked for...

Shirley was pleased to help. Rangi held the line while she went to check the files. Yes, there had been a complaint about Miss Kirby, and it had been investigated. But the investigation had come to nothing. The letter had been stamped, "No further action."

105

Rangi was really grateful. That would save him hours... and yeah, that'd mean he'd have time in the next week or so and they could... yeah, sure. He'd call her soon as.

He put the letters (in chromological order) and the list of victims' addresses in a folder in his case and went out to where Pike and the car waited.

So many people with guilty secrets... How many guilty secrets did *Rangi* know? Well, quite a lot, naturally, being in his job. Though by the time he got to learn them you could hardly call them secrets; most were on their way to becoming public property. But did he know anything about his nearest and dearest? Mum for instance? Don't make me laugh... But there was an awkward uncertainty; an uneasiness that he might never again be able just to accept people for what they were. Or rather, for what they seemed to be. For the first time Rangi's mind drifted round the possibilities of what those he knew *might* have lurking in their past... or even their present.

Poison pen... good name for them. Not just the victims, the way they made anyone who read them start thinking about their own folk. Poisoned you because there were so *many* of them. Some – most? – had to be true. So maybe there *were* things going on close to him... Hell, Rangi was buggered if he was going to start thinking the worst, to start letting that slow poison seep into *his* mind.

Maybe that was how cops – the ones who seemed to have a nose for a criminal – like Sir, for instance – maybe that was how they did it. Maybe they just thought the worst of people right from the start.

Maybe that's what Rangi should have been doing all these years.

...Like hell. He'd go on believing the best of people until they proved otherwise – like Mum was always saying. And he'd rely on his powers of observation – like Holmes. The hell with supposition and hunches.

He looked sideways at Pike. All those years at a private boys' school...

Sereyna Kirby was a frail little woman in a wheelchair. She must have been in her late sixties. Nice looking woman, but not the sort you'd think would be carrying on. *Could* people in wheelchairs carry on...? And at that age? Anyway, she didn't seem at all phased when Rangi introduced himself and Pike. "Detectives! My goodness, now what have I been up to?" Her teeth clicked as she chuckled. "Oh well, come in." She swung her chair round with practised agility, and with a couple of arm movements had propelled herself to an open doorway through which she vanished. Rangi and Pike followed.

The room was small, and dominated by the large desk with a typewriter and neat mounds of paper and books. Ms Kirby's chair was already beside the desk when Rangi got to the doorway. She nodded towards an elderly sofa covered with a crocheted rug. "Sit down." She glanced at the sheet of paper in her typewriter. "Ah well," she said and then added, "Now, I won't offer you a cuppa because I dare say you're very busy. How can I help you?"

Rangi hadn't realised until that moment how difficult the coming interviews were going to be. He couldn't bring Bradley's name into the conversation, of course – or not to start with, anyway – because the letters, after all, *had* been anonymous. If the victims didn't know who had written them that would be proof of their innocence.

...Of course, if they were guilty, they'd still *pretend* not to know who'd written them, wouldn't they. His stomach sank. What would you do now, Holmes?

"It's a bit of a delicate matter, eh," he said. He opened his case and took the printout of Bradley's letter to Income Support from the folder. "Um – it has come to our attention that ah Social Wel – I mean Income Support has received a –"

"Good God!" The blue eyes crackled with exasperation. "That stupid business all over again? About me and Simon Kerr?"

Rangi nodded. She might be old and fragile, but she was bloody intimidating.

"I am horrified that public money is being wasted on such a nonsense. The person they sent out to interview us said the case was closed and now here – *two* policemen, for pity's sake... the wages for two policemen, how much would that come to? For, say an hour. And the petrol – I don't imagine you walked here?"

Rangi shook his head.

"Altogether around $100, would you say? Must be. Where are the priorities? – no, no, not your doing, I dare say, but the whole thing is obviously ridiculous and the powers that be are *still*... However, now you are here, you can give me some advice. I didn't want to ring the police before, because I thought they were too busy about important matters. It would seem I was wrong, wouldn't it?"

Rangi opened his mouth and shut it again.

"I have been wondering what the legal position is. In my opinion Income Support is shielding a criminal. Surely the public must have some redress. Can I lay a complaint?" She paused.

"...Ah," said Rangi.

"Hmphh. You see, they *knew* – Income Support or whatever they're calling themselves knew. A woman – an investigator – came round. Simon and his wife were both here, and we explained the situation. Simon is a friend, a very dear friend. He gives his time freely to trundle me about the place – I've been in this thing since my teens – we read each other's work in manuscript – Sally, his wife, is a dear, but she's simply not interested in reading or in Simon's work. He takes me to meetings and launches and all that. But, as for jumping into bed with me and paying me for the privilege, the idea's insane!"

"Ah," said Rangi.

"And anyone who knew us would know that it's insane. But the letter had to be sent by someone who knew us, therefore the letter was deliberately malicious. In my opinion it contains criminal libel."

"Oh," said Rangi.

"And if it contains *criminal* libel, then the writer should be found and prosecuted."

Rangi nodded.

"The first step toward finding the writer would be to look at the writing or typing of the letter. But the Income Support people, while admitting the letter is malicious, refuse to release the original. They say they must protect their source, even when their source is plainly vicious. Is that, or is that not, abetting a crime by shielding the criminal?" The jaw snapped shut, the eyes sparked, the head craned forward.

"Ah..." said Rangi.

"Well then." Her mouth was a firm line, she nodded, folded her arms and sat back.

She seemed to have finished. "Ah," said Rangi.

"Indeed. Ah."

He waited, but she said no more. "Well," said Rangi. "What you said about the person who wrote the letter knowing you...?"

"It's obvious. Obvious on two counts. The first is that only someone who *knew* us both would know both our names. But there's more than that. The welfare people, although they wouldn't let us have the actual letter itself, let us have a copy that they'd typed out. It read-"

Rangi glanced at the printout in his hand. "*Sereyna Kirby, sickness beneficiary, is living in a de facto relationship with Simon Kerr and he supports her household.*"

"Now. Look at my name."

Rangi looked at it.

"It's plagued me all my life, that ridiculous spelling. In 1914, when girls were being given sensible names like Hilda and Margaret, my father insisted on calling me something that would mark me as different all my days. He –"

1914? She wasn't in her late sixties – she was over eighty! Eighty-year-olds didn't commit murder. Not even those who *weren't* in wheelchairs. You can forget this one, mate. Better get on to whoever's next on the list. What was she saying?

"...by someone who knew how my name was spelt. Very few people get it right. So whoever it was knew us. Which would mean that he or she would know that Simon is not only forty years younger than me, but happily married and simply a very obliging friend."

"Yeah," said Rangi. "Well, we better –"

"Now, it's not the libel that concerns me; the libel is important only because it is criminal and therefore is the means by which this sick person can be brought to justice. What concerns me is mainly that someone wanted me evicted from this flat –"

"Ah..." Rangi looked around. Comfortable, he reckoned, but pretty shabby. And small as.

"The only reason I can afford to live here is because, in addition to my superannuation I receive a disability allowance and a living-alone allowance. If the welfare people thought I was cheating on them, these allowances would be terminated and," the eyes were black with anger, "I would be on the street."

"Yeah –" Rangi began.

"And so that is the first thing that concerns me. The second is that someone of my acquaintance is – is a sick and vindictive person. I do not want to look at all my friends with suspicion. I need to *know* who is responsible."

"And you don't know?"

"Goodness me, man! What have I just been telling you? Now," the short white curls trembled with indignation, "what do you intend to do about it all?"

"Ah –"

Pike drove for a while in silence. Then he said, "Ooooof!"

"Yeah," said Rangi. He rubbed his hand slowly over his face and head. "Yeah." And after a while, "Well."

Pike turned a corner into a pleasant suburban street. "Number 29? Looks like it's down the other end."

"Just pull up here for a moment. I could do with another look at what Bradley said." Rangi realised that one hand was still gripping the printout of the letter about Miss Kirby. He scrumpled it into a side pocket of his case and took out the next one, tilting it so that Pike could see as well.

It was dated a couple of months previously and addressed to The Publisher, Bunnytime Books.

> *You should know that Patrick Darlington-Jones is at present under suspicion of being a member of a syndicate responsible for selling drugs to school children. For obvious reasons, the police do not wish this knowledge to be made public yet, but it was felt that, given the nature of Mr Darlington-Jones's work, it would be courteous to warn you of this matter. We expect you, in return, to respect the confidentiality of this information.*

"Nature of his work?" asked Rangi.

"He writes for kids. Big seller – you must have seen them, Sarge."

"Not that I know of."

"They're all the rage. *The Wormy World* they're called. Ah – Betty Butterfly, Cuthbert Chrysalis, Antonia Ant –"

"They're on TV! I've seen them. And on the ads – that thing about muesli..."

"Books, too. They're in all the shops. What about the drug thing, Sarge? Is it true? What did the narcs say?"

"Didn't ask them. They wouldn't tell me, anyway – have to keep everything under wraps until they can blow the lot. If it's a fib, they wouldn't tell me and if it's true – well," Rangi shifted uncomfortably, "they mightn't like the idea of us going round there right now, eh."

"You reckon there might be something in it?"

The surprise in Pike's voice made Rangi, who had reckoned just that (no smoke without fire, as Mum always said) think again. "Well," he said slowly, "you tell me."

Ashley realised this was one of those on-the-job test things that Sarge threw at him out of the blue every now and then. He took a deep breath. "Well, it sort of reads as though it could've come from the police, eh... Well, from the narcs, anyway."

Sarge grunted encouragingly.

"And it's not the sort of thing we'd be likely to do... Besides," Ashley suddenly realised this was the clincher, "how the hell would Bradley *know* if this guy was being investigated?"

"Good one." Sarge's solemn nod of approval was worth more than an A+ in any exam paper. "Now," Sarge said. "Think it through, mate. The thing's a lie, eh. Malicious, like Miss Kirby's one. But we have to find out whether this guy knows the letter was sent. And if he does know it was sent, does he know who sent it?"

Ashley waited; Sarge stared at the letter in silence for a while and then said, "So – how do we approach him?"

The question was casually asked, but Ashley was no fool. He realised Sarge had already got the whole thing figured out and was waiting to see if Ashley could do the same. Ashley felt hot and kept his head down in case he'd gone red.

Think! Either the guy knew about the letter or he didn't know. If he knew about the letter, then either he knew Bradley had sent it or he didn't know. If he knew Bradley had sent it either he'd killed him or he hadn't.

Brilliant logic, Ashley, but how the hell does that help decide how to approach the bugger?

Sarge was waiting.

What ways *were* there? They could either let the guy know they were cops or they could pretend to be something else. Nah – the stink would be higher than a month-old crayfish if it were found that they'd not only gone ahead on their own bat, but had impersonated members of the public in doing so. He guessed it *was* a crime to impersonate a member of the public...?

Sarge was waiting.

So they went in as police. Did they let the guy know about the letter, or not? If he didn't know about the letter, he wasn't the murderer. If he did know about the letter – God, Ashley had already been over all this...

Sarge was waiting.

Ashley stuck a pin into the whirligig of possibilities. "Shock tactics?" he said.

Sarge leant back. Then he punched Ashley lightly on the shoulder. "If you say so," he said. "Shock tactics it is."

Ashley grinned in relief.

The door was opened by a guy around his mid-twenties – big, good-looking and part Maori. However, Rangi's matey, "Kia ora," met with a heavy frostiness.

"I don't talk that stuff." The heavy body in torn shirt and oil-stained jeans stood squarely in the doorway. The hands were covered in grease, the face smeared with oil. "And if you're Mormons, sod off. I'm working."

"Not Mormons. Police." Rangi and Pike showed their identification. "We're looking for Patrick Darlington-Jones." Maybe the house had been sold or let – there was no way this beef-cake had thought up Betty Butterfly. Anyone – any *guy* – that wrote for the kiddies would be a bit like a grandfather, Rangi reckoned.

"That's me."

"*You?*"

"What I said." The full stare was hostile. He didn't ask what they wanted, didn't invite them in.

"Need to talk to you."

"So talk. But hurry. Like I said, I'm busy." Then he seemed to think better of it and sighed. "You might as well come through; I can listen while I work."

They followed him down a long, carpeted passageway where framed pictures of the fanciful creatures of *Wormy World* hung on the pastel pink paper and into a well-appointed modern kitchen where a young woman in a swimsuit was spooning something green into the mouths of two identical toddlers in identical high chairs. She glanced up as they entered and then returned to her task. The nearer twin peered round its mother's arm. "Dadadada!" it chuckled, green globs spraying wildly. Rangi reckoned wearing a swimsuit made sense.

Patrick Darlington-Jones appeared to find the display irresistible. He swerved from the course he had been making toward what was obviously the back door, and headed for the high chairs. "Gudday, gorgeous!" he boomed.

"Pad-*dy*!" protested the woman as he plucked the beaming toddler from its perch and held it high above his head, its arms and legs thrust out like a miniature sky diver. "She'll puke!"

But she didn't, she just gurgled a little green onto her father's chest and chortled happily. Her sister, entranced by the display, grinned upwards, green-splattered fists rubbing her temples in ecstasy. Patrick Darlington-Jones lowered the twin he was holding and with one hand loosened the feeding tray on the other's chair.

"Paddy!"

"They've finished, haven't they?" And, indeed, the bowl of green mush was almost empty, though Rangi doubted whether much was actually inside the twins.

With a daughter in each arm, Patrick Darlington-Jones swung round and round a few times, the twins shrieking in delight and pressing green cheeks against their father's oily face. In seconds a transfer of elements had taken place leaving all three faces and the twins' overalls smeared with an identical mixture of green and black.

The woman watched without expression until the twirling stopped. Then she said, "You messed 'em, you can have 'em. I'm going for a shower."

"Fine," he said. "Fine, fine, fine, fine." And he blew a raspberry into each twin's neck. "C'mon, then." He motioned with his head toward the back door which Pike hastened to open.

The door gave onto a large area paved with pink concrete cobblestones and roofed with green perspex. A partly dismantled Harley Davidson lay in a pool of oil in one corner. Patrick Darlington-Jones set his daughters on the ground, equipped each with a spanner and showed them how to use them to bash an empty oil can.

Once they were happily employed, he turned his attention to the bike. "Well?" he said.

"We'd like you to have a look at this." Rangi produced the letter to Bunnytime Books. He had to shout to get his voice over the row the kids were making.

Patrick Darlington-Jones glanced at the paper without taking it. "Too mucky," he yelled, his large hands delicately inserting a wire into a tube. "You read it to me."

Rangi tried, but after the third, "What was that again?" he gave up. "Doesn't matter if it gets messy," he said. "You read it."

Darlington-Jones swore as a wire sprang out of position, and glared at Rangi. "In a moment," he shouted.

They waited in a chaos of bangs and screams of delight. Finally the grease-smeared hands took the paper and Darlington-Jones gave it his attention.

Then he went mad. Hell, did he go mad! Even the twins stopped their drum bashing to stare open-mouthed at their father's rage. To start with, he got it wrong – he'd read the content of the letter and had not noticed who it was addressed to. So he got his wires crossed and decided that Rangi and Pike were there to arrest him for pushing drugs.

Once Rangi managed to get through to him that the dope squad did not suspect him of anything, and pointed out that the letter had been sent to his publisher, he went mad all over again. Even madder, if that were possible. The twins jumped up and down in delight. "DadadadaDA!" they yelled. A bathroom window that looked onto the paved area opened. "Jeez, Paddy! Put a sock in it!"

Once he had calmed down enough to be coherent, Patrick Darlington-Jones pulled a cell phone from his pocket, dialled and shouted for a while. Then he shoved the phone at Rangi. "Tell them!" he ordered. "Tell the gormless idiots that it's a bloody poison pen, that it's not true. I've been stewing for weeks over why I haven't got their bloody contracts... Tell the fuckwits!"

So Rangi told them.

And they wanted to know how he had a copy of the letter that had been sent them.

And he told them he was the police.

And they said that they only had his word for that and that as they were publishers of books for young people, which was a very responsible activity, they could not afford to have any breath of scandal –

And Patrick Darlington-Jones started yelling to tell the buggers and have done with it.

And Rangi said that there *was* no scandal.

And they asked why he was ringing them, then.

And the twins started their drum bashing again.

And he said that he was investigating another matter, a matter that had nothing to do with Mr Darlington-Jones, but had to do with the writer of the letter. It was, after all, a poison pen letter.

And Darlington-Jones shouted to stuff the sods.

And they said that was all well and good, but how did they know they were speaking to a police officer? They would need to ring Rangi's office and find out if there really were an officer by his name investigating poison pen letters.

And Rangi said they couldn't do that because the investigation was top secret. Not even his colleagues knew about it.

And they said that sounded very suspicious. But surely his superior officers would know about it.

And the twins' mother came out wrapped in a towel to see what the row was about and found that the twins each had a mouthful of nuts and bolts and she started yelling at Patrick.

And Rangi suddenly remembered that Sir was at that conference and said, of course his superior officer knew about it, and they could ring him. (This would mean that he had to get things straight before Sir got back in only three days, but it was really hard to think with all the noise.)

And then they asked to speak with Patrick Darlington-Jones again, but he was too busy fishing metal out of the twins' mouths so he shouted that he'd ring the buggers later.

Then Rangi and Pike left.

"Shock tactics worked okay, eh Sarge?" Pike said as he started the car. "He really didn't know about the letter, I reckon."

Rangi reckoned so, too.

"You didn't ask him who he thought might have sent it," Pike ventured.

Bugger. Well, how could he have – in the middle of all that? "That's right, I didn't," said Rangi.

Pike thought for a moment. "Yeah. No point, eh. Only get him wondering what we're on about and maybe talking to someone – to the murderer, even. That right, Sarge?"

"I reckon." He also reckoned that had better be the last call for the day because he needed to get showered and shaved and all that for the evening.

ten

They came laughing out of the restaurant into the pleasantly cool night air. It had been an exhilarating evening; Julia was entranced, delighted, terrified by the trickiness of his mind. He would be burbling on about Rugby League for all the world like the big macho hulk he looked, and then she'd catch the gleam in his eye – he was thinking about something worlds away from football. It was a gleam of sheer intelligence, a betrayal of his enjoyment of power – a hint that he was amused by the situation as well. She was sure she read him right and trod most warily, working her hardest to be an amusing dinner companion.

She hadn't done too badly. She could make him laugh, and from time to time something more than just amused intelligence shone from his eyes. Several times he had grinned at her and said something outrageous, something so outspokenly bald, so overstepping the mark that he might as well have said plainly, "You haven't got a hope, woman. I can say – can *do* – what I like because of what I know about you. I want you, you know what's coming, you got no choice."

So when, as they reached his car, he slid a hand down round her bottom and pulled her close to him, bending her backward, an arm round her upper back steadying her so she didn't quite fall, she was ready to surrender then and there if that was what he demanded. Their mouths met, she allowed her tongue to dart, to flirt. He whispered something that sounded like *Wheeeee* and the next thing she was lying back over the bonnet of the car with his hand urgently scooping her breast.

He only just managed to stop. Jeez, imagine the headlines – COP HAS IT OFF IN MAIN STREET. Imagine Sir's outraged sarcasm. Pike's admiring grin.

"Sorry," he muttered. "Reckon we better wait a few minutes, eh."
He helped her stand upright and stepped back still holding her hand.
The look in her eyes nearly made him start all over again. He unlocked
the car and opened the door for her, stroking her shoulder as she
moved past him into the seat. He got behind the wheel and sat for
a little while to get his breath back. "Your place or mine?" he asked
– she'd told him she'd taken a motel room so that she wouldn't have
to drive back to Auckland late.

"Has to be yours. My car's there."

"Oh yeah, I forgot." He started the car.

...His place was a bit of a mess at the moment and he didn't want
to spoil things. The evening so far had been perfect – she was a
wonderful listener, and obviously genuinely keen on sport. And she
was really witty, too – he'd never laughed so much. She'd kept him
guessing, though. Every time he'd given her a look that should let her
know what he was thinking, she'd done a sort of gasp thing and
looked away. He'd dropped the odd hint – subtly, of course – in the
conversation, but she hadn't taken him up on any of them. In fact,
he hadn't been certain till just now, by the car. The way her tongue...
and the way she'd looked at him... Rangi's foot pressed harder on the
accelerator.

A memory of stacked and unstacked dishes, furry circles floating
in half-empty cups, beer cans on the carpet, the unmade bed and the
clothes that needn't be picked up till wash-day. The car slowed. "Tell
you what," he said.

"What?"

"We collect your car and I follow you round to the motel."

"If you like."

"It's just that – well, I don't want you having to get up and leave
in the wee small hours, eh."

Her hand was on his knee. "That's kind of you," she said.

Wheeeeeee!

Julia realised that his coming to her bed was of a piece with his power.
He would be the one to decide when to stay and when to leave. When
to come and when to go.

...When to come, God! Julia had never had a night like it; the time
with Freddie paled into nothingness beside this. Freddie's lack of skill
had disappointed; Rangi, after his first rapture, had been a wonderful,
interested lover. And always there was the added piquancy of his

117

power over her. *If I do not please this man,* she said to herself with gleeful apprehension, *he may well arrest me. He has the power to arrest me even if I do please him.* She did everything she could think of to gratify him and got as good as she gave.

They drifted to sleep, woke sticky and ardent, and slept again. Sometime during the night he made her promise to come back in a few days. Stay on after the funeral, maybe.

"The funeral?"

He smiled and stroked her cheek. "You're half asleep. Yeah, the funeral, dozy. You'll be coming down for that, eh? Being his agent."

"Oh. Yes, yes of course." Shit, she'd have to. "When is it?"

"Not certain, but the inquest's Monday – they'll release the body then. So it'll be Tuesday, probably. Want me to ring and let you know?"

"Please."

"And you stay on. I'll get the flat cl –, get some really good kai in, and we'll make a night of it at my place," he said.

She agreed. She had no choice of course.

It was a real struggle for Rangi to get up in the morning. Not because he hadn't had much sleep, it wasn't sleep he was wanting. But he'd told Pike to pick him up from the flat at nine, so he'd have to get going. Bloody hell – it *was* a day off, after all. Maybe he could just ring Pike and... that publishing guy was going to get in touch with Sir soon as he got back from his conference. Shit. Rangi put one foot out of bed.

She stirred.

He put his foot back in the bed and turned to her.

She stilled.

He touched her cheek, gently pushing back a long strand that had strayed into the corner of her mouth.

She smiled and opened her eyes.

...He made it to his flat just as Pike was getting back into a car.

"Hey!" he yelled.

"Gudday, Sarge." Pike closed the car door and walked back toward the drive.

"Been waiting long?" Rangi asked.

"Not long," said Pike. "Saw your car wasn't there, so I reckoned something might've come up."

Rangi grinned. "Something did," he said. "Several times."

"Eh? I looked for a note, but..."

"Yeah, well I didn't leave one. Reckoned I'd be back before you got here. Come on, mate, in you get; we better get this show on the road. No trouble getting a car?"

"There were loads of spare ones. I just signed it out for both of us. Called it 'Research'."

"Good one. I'll drive seeing it's unofficial."

The next name on the list was another writer. Rangi sighed. He hadn't had much luck with writers yet. He got Pike to read the letter out while he drove. It had been sent to a Miss Phyllis Teasedale.

"Heard of her," said Pike.

"Yeah?"

"Writes historical fiction."

"That right?

I was interested to hear that Mrs Barbara Quentin is of the opinion that the funds of the Society of Authors dwindled alarmingly during your time as Treasurer. She spoke of it at considerable length at the last S of A meeting, which is strange as I had thought that you were close friends. If you continue to choose your friends paying more attention to their ability to flatter than to their loyalty, you might be wise not to be absent from future meetings.

"Hell," said Rangi. "Well, we better see this Mrs Quentin."

"Yeah," Pike agreed. "Shock tactics again, Sarge?"

"What you reckon?"

"Worked okay last time, eh."

So Rangi showed Mrs Quentin the letter as soon as they had presented their credentials. "Oh dear," she said. "Oh dear, oh dear, oh dear. You'd better come in." They followed her through thickly carpeted rooms decorated with original paintings, pots, bronzes, paper fans and decorated boomerangs, and into a sunny "conservatory" containing ferns, chairs, bookcases, tables and a desk with a computer. Through an open door they were conscious of another presence, an occasional cough, rustle of newspaper, shuffle of slippers on carpet. "My husband," Mrs Quentin said as she caught Rangi's inquiring glance. "Ever since he retired he's fidgeted if he doesn't know where I am or what I'm doing. I daren't shut the door, Chester would be so upset. But he's hard of hearing, poor love, so we can talk quite openly."

119

She sat on a cane sofa and waited till Rangi and Pike had each settled themselves on matching chairs before she began. "You'll have come about that dreadful man. I've been half expecting you ever since I heard of his death. You'll have realised that he's the one who wrote that." Her hand trembled slightly as she pointed to the letter in Rangi's hand. "And... not *quite* untrue, that's the cleverness of it. It is true that I admire Phyl – well, she's such a wonderful writer, isn't she?"

"Historical fiction," said Rangi.

"Well, there's nothing wrong with that, I hope?"

"No. Course not. Just thought... I mean, she's known, eh."

"A household name. But this letter – I probably do chatter on about her more than I should, but – I'm just a scribbler, you know, only an affiliated member, not a *real* writer at all, though I have had some things – just little ones – in the paper and a few magazines... and the fact that she and I are friends, well, I *do* feel it's an honour and so I... but you see, the very first time we met, well, something *clicked*, you know how it is, and she's often round here for a meal and she's come to me at odd little times when she – writers don't earn very much money, you know, even the best of them, and Phyl is certainly one of the best if not *the* best in this country.

"So that's true, you see. And I *did* mention when we were talking and she wasn't at that meeting, but everyone knows that that was the year our branch hosted the AGM and whatever you try to do to keep costs down things can get out of hand so easily and the catering alone. So Chester and I helped out and everything was all right and what happened at the meeting was just that I said that the next AGM's ours again and perhaps something in the nature of a levy might be a good idea considering what happened last time.

"And that dreadful man was there of course and he heard the discussion and turned it all upside down and into this thing and when Phyl got back, she goes to speak everywhere round the world you know – I sometimes tell her she's one of our principal exports! – when she got back and read it she was round here straight away, she's like that it's all 'up front' as they say with Phyl – and of course I told her what had happened and how it had happened and of course she understood and she stayed on to dinner in fact, well she would have but Chester and I were only going to have an omelette and so we all went out to eat at a restaurant."

The red head which had been nodding from time to time in emphasis gave an extra vehement shake to signify the end of the explanation and the lined face set in an expression of anxious enquiry as if to ask if there was anything else that the policemen needed to know.

The thing that Rangi needed to know was why she was so certain that the letter writer was Joseph Bradley.

"Well, he was there, you see, and it was a very nasty night, a really very nasty night and not many turned out at all. Phyl was in the States, of course, being our principal export as I often tell her, and there were only a handful. Let's see, there'd have been, well Wallace was there because he never misses, being the Chairperson, and Trevor who's Secretary, then there was me of course and that bald young woman who can't speak without using *words*, but they say that her work's very good even if, well it's a bit robust for my taste though very worthy I'm sure, but it is surprising that publishers will... anyway, who am I to talk, being only affiliated?... and it couldn't be her because if there's one thing you can say about that dreadful letter, it's that it's written in good English, and it wouldn't have been Wallace or Trevor –"

"Why not?"

"Because they're not the sort, there isn't an ounce of malice in either of them, I often tell them they're not the tiniest bit like real writers. Besides they both write by hand and transfer it to a typewriter; they hate computers and this was written on a computer, wasn't it? And who else was there? Oh, there were the two ladies from out of town, they come every time. Fixtures, I call them, they come just for the glory of mixing with real writers though Phyl hardly notices them at all, they've had nothing published, of course. Well, *they* wouldn't have written it. It could only be that dreadful man, and Phyl agrees with me."

"Yes, well. Well, you could be right. It could be Mr Bradley that wrote it. So now I need to know what you were doing on the night of the 15th."

"You mean it was murder?" The blue painted lids disappeared entirely into the powdered wrinkles under the eyebrows as Mrs Quentin's eyes opened wide. Rangi cursed. "Someone killed him deliberately?"

"Very probably not. We're treating it as a hit and run, but it's just we got to make enquiries in a case like this. And may I ask you not to divulge any of the matters spoken about here to anyone."

"Oh no. Oh, of course not. I'm not a chatterer. And if it *is* murder and I talked about it I might give the show away to the guilty person, mightn't I?"

"Exactly," said Rangi. "Now, I do need to know what you were doing last Monday."

"Ah, I've an alibi for that! And what's more, I can give Phyl one as well. We were both in Wellington."

"Wellington?"

"It was the AGM of the Society of Authors. The next one's ours, as I think I mentioned. Phyl wasn't going to go, but these things are such fun and you meet so many... there's a dinner, you see, and guest speakers and lots of discussion at the meetings of course, and anyway I persuaded Phyl and we stayed at this hotel – there weren't many writers staying there unfortunately, they seemed on the whole to go for cheaper places but I hadn't thought – anyway, it was great fun and Phyl and I asked people, Johnny Canning came back to drinks so it almost seemed that the AGM was being held at the hotel someone said, I think it was Sir Neville. Anyway we were still there on Monday, actually lots from here stayed on because there was a launch at the Beehive on the Monday evening..."

How the hell could they stop this flow without being rude? Sir would be back the day after tomorrow and Rangi had told the publisher on the phone that Sir knew all about the poison pen thing... and the list of those to interview was so long. There was a dull ache in his stomach. Christ, they *had* to get through the list in the next two days. He raised his eyebrows to signal Pike it was time to be going – rude or not.

Ashley caught Sarge's signal and understood in a flash that there was something they should be asking. Something this woman knew or might know that could help them. Sarge would ask about it sure enough, if Ashley didn't. But he was giving Ashley first go. The fact that they were off duty probably helped – it didn't matter if things got mucked up and it all took a bit more time than usual – Jeez, he was lucky; Sarge was grabbing every chance he could for on-the-spot training. But what could it be she knew...? Of course! "The other people at the AGM..." said Ashley.

She blinked, startled, blocked by an unexpected dam. "I beg your pardon?"

"I don't suppose you could give us a list of local members who went down to Wellington for the AGM?"

"Of course I could. The minutes arrived yesterday. Now..." She stood up and went to a mahogany filing cabinet. "Here we are." From a folder she extracted a few pages. "Would you like a copy?"

"Ah – yeah. Yes, thank you," said Sarge. "If it's no trouble." He grinned his approval at Ashley, and Ashley grinned back.

"This is one of my little weaknesses." Mrs Quentin took a patchwork cover off what Ashley had thought was a small table to reveal a compact photocopier. "Of course, the fax copies things, but it doesn't produce nearly so pleasant a result. Phyl, was *very* scathing when this arrived, I can tell you." She chuckled. "But I know which one of us gets more use out of it!"

Finally they were back in the car comparing the list of those present at the Society of Authors AGM in Wellington with the list of poison pen letters. "Great." Sarge scratched a line through four of the names. "That's saved us a fair bit of time. Only one left is this Secretary guy. The one with the drama club, and he's not the next – not if we're going chromo-logical." Ashley grinned at the deliberate malapropism. Sarge added, "Good thinking, mate."

Sarge was bloody generous – pretending that he hadn't tipped Ashley the wink to start with. Still, Ashley had learnt the hard way that it was no use trying to thank him for this sort of thing. Sarge always pretended to have not the faintest idea of what Ashley was on about.

Rangi was relieved to be shot of writers for the time being. They were difficult people to talk to. "Who's next?" he asked.

"Francis Piper. He's at the university. He's got a Fellowship there – the letter's the one that questions his academic record."

Shit. Rangi had had dealings with university types before. They were almost as bad as writers. However, it turned out that Francis Piper was not at home. On a research trip overseas, his landlady said. And what's more he'd been overseas for some time so that ruled *him* out.

"There won't have been any truth in it, anyway," Pike said when they were back in the car. "Universities have got to be really careful about academic records and all that. This one's another sheer spite one I reckon."

"They all have been so far, eh." *Well, Watson, it's fairly obvious that if all but one of the letters turn out to have no truth in them, the one that is truthful was probably written about our murderer.*

123

Why, Holmes?
Shut up, Watson.
"Where now?" Rangi asked.
"In chromo-logical order?" What was Pike grinning at?
"In chromo-logical order."
Pike chuckled. "The one to the tax department."

Barton and Banks, estate agents, of Marlin Street, are regularly concealing around 20% of the revenue they receive as commission on sales.

Rangi thought for a while. "Let's leave it. Too many people in an estate agents. Besides, there won't be anyone there. If any of them are working on a Sunday they'll be at Open Homes. Save it up in case we don't get lucky with any of the others."

"Then the next one is Waldorf McCarthy. I think he's from the University too, Sarge. Teaches English."

Well, with luck he'd be overseas as well. *What are you trying to do, Holmes? Eliminate all the suspects?*

Eliminate the impossible, Watson, and what is left, however improbable, will be the truth.

What does that mean in this case, Holmes?

Shut up, Watson.

"Read us the letter again," Rangi said.

I feel it is important to point out to you that your husband's interest in his teenage daughter is unwholesome. You may not be aware that he is meeting her at various venues outside the family home.

The McCarthys' was a pleasant, largish house with a trio of skateboarding youths on the sloping drive. "They're round the back," one of them yelled before Rangi had a chance to ask for McCarthy.

Round the back a large man and a tiny woman, both in tattered shorts and shirts were improvising a table, carefully lowering an old door onto two piles of bricks. The woman looked over her shoulder as they came round the corner of the house and called, "Hi. Won't be a moment – the drinks are in the kitchen. Through the back door and turn right – we'll be with you in a moment." She picked up a couple of table cloths from a covered barbecue and flicked them out over the door. She was in her late thirties, Rangi reckoned, but she had good legs. "Put a brick on each corner, Wald, to weight them till I get things out."

But the man moved to her and said something. "Oh." She tucked a strand of hair back behind her ear. "Sorry. Thought you were students." Her smile was nice. "Horribly early students."

"No. Sorry to interrupt." Rangi introduced himself and Pike. "It's obviously an awkward time, but if you could give us a few minutes, Mr McCarthy..."

"It's urgent?"

Rangi nodded.

"Oh. Well then, come in."

They sat at the dining table. In the kitchen next door there was the noise of cutlery, a fridge door. Pike got up and closed the door. McCarthy's eyebrows rose.

"Just to start with, Sir, I'd like to speak to you privately."

"Someone's in trouble?"

"Don't know. Have you ever seen this?"

Shock tactics again. McCarthy took the sheet of paper, glanced at it and said, "Hell!"

"Well?"

"Of course I've seen it – the sick product of a sick mind. Maggs showed it to me as soon as it arrived. Nothing in it – she knew there was nothing in it, of course – but naturally she was upset, and – just as naturally, I suppose, though it hurt – she... well, she wondered... Anyway, I dropped a hint about it to some of them at work and a couple had a word with me. They'd had the same sort of thing. Well, it stuck out a mile who must be sending them. I got the two chaps who'd had problems – Jones and Hancock, I dare say they're on your list, too – to come round one evening and have a chat to Maggs. Cleared it up. Not that she'd ever really believed..."

He gave a half-hearted smile. "The *really* sick thing is what it's done to poor little Izzy. And me. I just can't feel natural with her any more. Can't – you know – give her a cuddle or anything, the sort of thing fathers just do. She hasn't any idea why, of course, and it's puzzling her. The poor kid hasn't talked about how she must be feeling, but she's trying everything to be specially helpful, wants my attention all the time. I can give her the odd hug when Maggs or the boys are there, but when there's just the two of us – well, I feel awkward. And it shows." He sighed. "So, these have turned up in

Bradley's effects, eh, and you're checking to see if anyone did him in?"

"Ah –"

"Well, *I* didn't. To my mind he needed a doctor not an executioner. Though I can understand... I mean, what's happened here is bad enough, but in the end it's not going to change our lives all that much. Jones and Hancock's marriages are ruined, and then there's poor young Robby Hale. God only knows what other damage Bradley did."

Rangi had a quick glance at the letters remaining in the file. Jones, Hancock, Hale were all there. So Jones and Hancock were university types, too. He'd known from the content of the letter that Hale was. If only all university types were as easy to talk to as McCarthy. "Would you like to tell me about these others?" he asked.

"That would be quite inappropriate." The large face was no longer affable, the eyes were cold. "I don't gossip, and you'll find they are quite able to tell you their own experiences. Apart from Hale, naturally."

"Hale?"

"He committed suicide some months ago and is therefore unlikely to have gone on to homicide, which requires a certain amount of corporeal substance to effect."

Rangi gave a mental shrug. This sort of language was much more like what he expected from academics. Stuff him. "Of course." He made his voice stiff and cool. "Now, Sir. I need to know where you were last Monday evening."

"Monday!" A short bark of laughter. "Mondays I do my stint to lessen my time in Purgatory. On Mondays Maggs drags me off to Bridge Club for two and a half hours and spends the following five hours or so telling me what I did wrong – hand by excruciating hand. In the words of the immortal Ashford, I *offer it up as a mortification.*"

"So you were there for three hours – starting...?"

"Seven-thirty sharp."

"Could you give me the names of some of the people at the club, Sir?"

He could. Rangi would get Pike to do a bit of checking, of course, but it was clear that Waldorf McCarthy was not guilty of anything. Anything at all.

Rangi glanced at his watch. "Time for one more before lunch. Who's next?"

The next letter was addressed to the Board of Trustees of a local high school.

It is known that Mr Trevor Illingby, a member of your Staff, is using the drama club as a screen for activities which, given the ages of the lads involved, are criminal.

"Getting back in time a bit, Sarge. This one's dated well over a year ago."

"If it's murder, mate, it took some planning, and planning takes time." But Rangi was worried. *He* couldn't keep mad at someone for over a year – not mad enough to kill, anyway. Would *anyone* store up resentment as long as that? "That's the one who's in the Authors thing, isn't it? The one who didn't go down to Wellington?"

"Yeah. Secretary."

And the old girl with the money had said Trevor hadn't an ounce of malice in him.

"If he's the Secretary, why wasn't he down there with the rest of them?"

"You reckon he might have been busy running someone over, Sarge?"

"You never know." Rangi sighed; he wasn't very hopeful.

However, Trevor Illingby was nervous, which was a good sign. He was nervous opening the door even, and when he realised he was being visited by the police, he was even more nervous. He ushered them into his living room and sat them down, then took a chair opposite and made an obvious effort to get himself under control. "Excuse me," he said, "I'm slightly asthmatic." He struggled for a little while, then said, "No good," took a spray from his pocket, inhaled, and visibly relaxed. "Sorry," he said. "Sorry." A pathetic attempt at a smile. "I must be allergic to police!" He gave up trying to smile. "What's the matter? Why have you...?"

Rangi had the letter ready in his hand, but he thought better of it. Shock tactics might be a bit much for this one; Rangi didn't want the guy collapsing or anything, especially seeing this was unofficial. Hell, Senior Sergeant or not he'd be out on his ear at best; might even be dragged through the courts – and young Pike with him.

...Unless, of course, it turned out that this guy was the murderer. "Just a few questions, Sir, about – well, about the drama club to start with."

"The *drama* club?" Neat dark eyebrows rose over brown eyes. A slight pink flushed under the olive skin. Whatever he'd been expecting, this wasn't it.

"Ah, yeah. You run the drama club at the school, don't you?"

"Yes. Well – yes I do, I suppose..."

"You suppose?"

"Well, it's not really... It's moribund, I'm afraid –"

"Ah?"

"Almost defunct."

"Oh."

"There hasn't been a meeting in months. It was going so well just a short time ago, and then... well, students – a lot of them – just stopped coming..."

"Why would that be?"

"I don't know, but I used to get very annoyed because the Phys Ed Department seemed always to be dropping in and sorting out equipment... I have to use the gym, you see, because there isn't any drama facility, and Tuesdays is drama club we agreed and it's supposed to be sacrosanct. But when I mentioned it to the Head, he – well, he was most..." The flush was deepening.

"He was most...?"

There was anger and bafflement in the voice now. "He said he'd *told* the Phys Ed to drop in and keep and eye on things. As if the drama group would break any of their stupid equipment, or want to steal anything! And when I said what nonsense that was, he said that stealing wasn't the sort of activity he was meaning, and if I didn't know what he was talking about, that was all well and good. And now *you're* here asking about the club –. Oh God, they weren't doing drugs, were they?"

"No, Sir."

"What *is* it about then?"

"Ah -"

"Surely I have the right to know? If something was going on under my nose – and there's the other thing, the way they're avoiding me at the school... as though I were a germ that's caught penicillin... This last year has not been easy, I can tell you. I don't want to think I'm paranoid, but it's either that or people are talking about me – conversations change as I come into the room, that sort of thing. So what is it? What is it about?"

"I'm not actually in a position to tell you at the moment, Sir."

128

Rangi was thinking fast. The guy *seemed* to know nothing, but he was an actor, eh. You didn't run a school drama club without being an actor yourself. Rangi remembered the end-of-year staff concerts at his old school where Mr Taylor, who ran the drama club, used to have the whole school in bloody stitches he was that funny. Fantastic actor. He did comic songs dressed up as music hall character, and once he played this old charlady with a scarf round her head and a fake nose with Mr Taylor's moustache curling around underneath, and a pigtailed girl in blue school uniform carrying a soccer ball and a teddy bear... "It's – ah – sensitive information at the moment."

"Sensitive in –!" The signs of stress that had lifted after Illingby had used the inhaler, were back again. His voice trembled. "Well then, what is it you want to know about the drama club?"

"Not the drama club, Sir."

"*Not* – ?"

"I'd like you to tell us, Sir, of your movements Monday night last."

"My-" Now it was not just the voice that was trembling. "What *is* this? Am I being accused of something? I think I have a right – surely I have a right..." The guy was fighting to control his shaking. Shit, now he'd started talking about rights, they could be really in it. Off duty, no orders to act as they were doing, using the fact that they were police to intimidate... All the bugger needed to do was pick up the phone and ask a few questions and it was goodbye to a promising career. Rangi glanced at Pike and jerked his head toward the door; the sooner they got out of there the better.

Ashley realised what Sarge was wanting and acted quickly. The guy was nearly hysterical, he could make a bolt for it at any moment. Ashley stood up and stretched to give the impression that he needed some exercise and then strolled across the room to the door – do nothing to alarm a suspect who is showing signs of instablility. He stood leaning back casually, blocking Illingby's escape route. He'd already noted that all windows in the room had burglar latches which prevented their being opened any further than they already were.

His move had distracted the suspect whose white face jerked round toward Ashley. Sarge was pretending to be surprised as well, and there was a silence that Ashley felt compelled to fill. His gaze fell on the open garage. "You got a new Toyota, eh?" he said.

Illingby spluttered.

"Toyota?" said Sarge. "What colour?"

"Red," Ashley said. His stomach was flipping with excitement; he managed to keep his voice calm, though. Said it coolly. "A new red Toyota. Mind if I take a look?"

"What is this? Who are you really?"

"Like we said, Sir," said Sarge who had crossed to the window to look at the garage. "Just making a few inquiries." His nod told Ashley to get out there and check that car over.

Ashley didn't need telling twice. He was outside and into the garage like a flash. There was a wide window in the back wall of the garage and he could see clearly all round the car. Try as he might he couldn't see a single dent or scratch in the thick glossy paintwork. Would there have been time for a panelbeater to return the bodywork to such pristine condition? This was Sunday. The earliest the car could have got to a workshop if it had been involved in Monday's night's killing, would have been Tuesday morning. That gave at most five days to undent, repaint – and to make a job as perfect as this. Besides, all panelbeaters had been checked, and none had reported fixing a red Toyota. He left to take the bad news back to Sarge. As he came out of the garage he could see Sarge watching him through the window. Ashley shook his head. Sarge shrugged.

And it turned out that Illingby had an alibi for that night, anyway. Sarge had got it out of him while Ashley had been checking the Toyota. He'd had a bad attack of asthma and a neighbour had run him into the nearest Accident and Emergency clinic. He'd been there from just after eight until nearly ten. When Ashley came in, Sarge made a quick phone call – the A and E confirmed the times.

Rangi half expected Illingby to have a go at them once he was in the clear, and he wasn't looking forward to fielding more awkward questions about what Rangi and Pike were doing. But the poor bugger was so wrought up and so grateful to be seeing them off the premises that it didn't seem to cross his mind that he might have a grievance against the police.

"Lunch break," Rangi said as he started the car. "But I got a phone call to make first. There's a phone box."

"Why not use the car phone, Sarge?"

"It's a private call," said Rangi self-righteously.

He was just about to hang up when she answered. Breathless. And – he grinned – she sounded even more breathless when she heard who was calling.

"I – I've just this minute got in."

"Yeah. Yeah, reckoned that was it. Good trip?"

More breathlessness. A laugh? "I didn't notice."

"No?"

"I had too much to... to think about."

"I know the feeling. Hell, I'm back to work and it's extra hard yakker having to keep my mind on the job, eh."

A laugh.

"So I reckoned I'd better give you a ring." He grinned again. "That is, assuming you do *want* to talk...?"

"I – I have a choice?"

He noticed Pike looking at the phone box and turned round to hide his grin. "You got no choice at all," he said. "I reckon neither of us got any choice about this thing."

"*Neither* of us?"

He got the message, *don't be too sure of yourself, mate.* "Well, one of us hasn't, anyway," he said, and then, to fill the silence, "You coming down to the inquest tomorrow?"

"No – I – I hadn't intended to. Should I?"

Rangi thought. The inquest could take most of the morning, but he'd be sitting round waiting, not able to talk to her. Then back to work for a few hours and then he and Pike really ought to carry on with these interviews. Try to get everyone done before Sir got back on... on Wednesday. Wednesday – the day after the funeral. She was spending Tuesday night with him. When the hell would he get time to clean up the flat? Maybe Mum... And with Sir around it'd be really hard to go on looking for the murderer. Hell, with Sir back, he'd need to have found the murderer already...

"Do you think I should?"

"Eh?"

"Should come to the inquest?"

"No, probably no need. Just the funeral. I'll wangle the rest of the funeral day off with luck."

"Good. I'll look forward to it."

"Me too – hey, we're looking forward to a funeral!"

"So we are!"

Her voice was so close, so warm, it was as though she was in the booth with him. He leaned on the wall and closed his eyes. "Julia," he said.

"Yes?"

"Nothing. Just saying your name. It's a nice name, eh?"

There was a knocking on the door of the phone box. Rangi opened his eyes. Pike. Mouthing, "You okay?" Rangi nodded. "Look," he said, "I got to go. See you Tuesday."

"What time?"

"Eh?"

"What time is the funeral?"

"Not sure. I'll let you know."

Lunch was a couple of pies eaten as they drove. The next two letters had been sent concerning people who had left town. Pike could check tomorrow that they hadn't popped back for a spot of homicide. The letter before those two – chromologically – was about a junior lecturer called Robert Hale. It had been sent to the University Council.

Robert Hale has falsified the marks for one of his paramours. It would be advisable for you to check the script (English 169) of Marcus Brownley. It is not possible for a candidate of Brownley's mediocre talents to attain any grade higher than C. He has been awarded an A-, which is clearly beyond his abilities. I would suggest that you check all of Hale's marking; there may be others of his friends who have acquitted themselves suspiciously well.

"This is the guy Mr McCarthy mentioned," Rangi said. "The one that committed suicide. We can cut *him* off our list."

Ashley noticed the slight emphasis on the pronoun and leapt to it. (You had to be quick to pick up Sarge's hints.) "Rule *him* out, you mean, but not necessarily family and friends?"

Sarge nodded thoughtfully, then sighed. "Yep," he said. "Right on. Let's go looking for family and friends."

eleven

"Looks a bit shut up," said Pike as they pulled into the kerb outside the tidy, brick two-storey where Robert Hale had lived with his parents. "Too hot to have all the windows shut; they could be away."

It seemed they were. No answer to the front door chimes, no answer to the knock on the back door.

"Neighbours?" said Pike.

"Neighbours."

Mrs Next-door was home. Yes, she knew the Hales. Knew them well. But no, they weren't at home; they were in Australia having a bit of a break. Mrs Next-door herself was keeping an eye on the place, collecting the mail and all that. The family had recently suffered a terrible tragedy and Bren had taken it especially hard. It was their son, young Robby – a lovely, lovely boy, and their only one – and he- Oh, they knew about that already? Friends of the family, were they? Just dropping in? Well, something like that scars you for life, doesn't it? This trip was the first time Bren, poor love, had shown any interest in doing anything. They'd been away for just on a week now – left last Monday for Auckland to catch a morning flight over to Oz on Tuesday. What time did they leave Monday? Oh, around two o'clock. Bren was almost excited, they were staying the night in a really posh hotel, not just a motel. Starting off with a real good hotel meal with all the trimmings, Bren had said. The Excelsior. Mrs Next-door's sister had stayed there once and said it was really lovely. Bob wasn't sparing any expense. Of course, they were quite well off...

They were going to be away for another week. "I'll tell them you called," said Mrs Next-door. "What name shall I say?"

"Ah – Roberts."

"Mr Roberts. I'm sure they'll be sorry to have missed you. You wouldn't like to leave them a note?"

"No need. Thanks all the same."

"Should we check the hotel, Sarge?" asked Pike.

"Better, I suppose." But Rangi didn't hold out much hope. "Better find out if there were any friends who might've done it, too. Leave that till tomorrow, but. Then we can look up this..." he looked at the letter, "this Marcus Brownley and ask about his A-. The uni will have his address seeing he's a student."

"So it's Jones and Hancock now?"

"I reckon."

"We're getting through them pretty quick, Sarge."

"Too bloody quick."

It is possible that you are still unaware of what is common knowledge on Campus. Crispin Jones and Stephanie Lawder, the English Department Secretary, have been lovers for some considerable time. It might be advisable to check on whether your husband really is attending all the evening meetings he claims to attend.

"Yeah," said Rangi. "That's the double letter. Two the same, only one's about Crispin Jones and one's about Hector Hancock. Both supposed to be having it off with the secretary. The bugger sent both letters off on the same day about the same woman, so I reckon there's not going to be much truth in it, eh."

"Which one first?"

"Jones. He's the closest."

Mrs Jones was pretty but a bit too skinny. Her face closed down when she heard it was her husband that Rangi and Pike were wanting to talk to, but she cheered up when she realised they were police, and parted readily enough with his present address. "If he's in," she said, "you could remind him he's nearly a month behind with the payments. Point out that his children aren't pining for him so much that they've stopped needing to eat."

"Well..." Rangi began, but the door was already shut. Rangi raised his eyebrows at Pike. "Marriage," he said. "Hell."

Pike was looking at him oddly. Rangi rearranged his face and got into the car.

Crispin Jones's flat was small, modern, one of a block of four. Jones himself, mid-thirties, dark and handsome, opened the door. Rangi, using shock tactics again, introduced himself and Pike and handed

134

over the letter. Jones grimaced as he recognised it. "Come in," he said, and led them into a kitchen-dining-sitting room where a cute looking red-headed girl in shorts and shirt was watching a film on television. "Can you turn that down, Poppet, or watch it in the bedroom? We need to talk."

The girl turned green eyes fringed with black towards them for a moment, shrugged and reached forward for a set of headphones. The television sound ceased as she plugged them in and settled back to continue watching.

Jones grinned apologetically at Rangi and pointed to the dining table. "We can sit here." Then, without waiting till they had settled, he added, "I half thought there might be some questions asked when Bradley was run over. Seemed too fortunate an accident. I take it you're thinking it might be more than a hit-and-run?"

"Not really," said Rangi. "We just got to check a few things out, though. Be on the safe side, you know. But it's interesting, Mr Jones, that you think it might be something more than just an accident."

"Well, if you've found that," Jones nodded at the letter, "you've no doubt found others. It was obvious the guy was sending them out wholesale; a nasty customer. Merilyn got that one, Heck's wife – Hector Hancock – got another. Waldo McCarthy. And Robby Hale... I spoke to his father, the University Council was investigating something... Robby was a nice chap, but... well, there must've been some truth in it or he wouldn't have done away with himself like that."

"Was there truth in this one?"

"About me and Steph? Well, yes." He glanced over to where the girl was sitting immersed in the film. "But as for her having it off with old Heck at the same time, that's a laugh. Bradley wrote identical letters, did you know? Merilyn blew up and I didn't bother to try to do anything – we'd been frazzling each other for years, anyway. And Steph was anxious for me to make her an honest woman, as the saying goes. The sad thing was that Bronwyn Hancock refused to believe the letter about Heck was a lie. I think she'd been wanting a chance to get rid of him and, even when Steph and I went round to see her, she wasn't intending to listen. Poor old Heck was really cut up about it at the time."

"You and Mr Hancock talked about the letters your wives had received?"

"Of course. And Waldo talked about his – Bradley was a worm, suggesting a thing like that. I don't know if there were any others, but there could well have been."

"You were all certain that Joseph Bradley was the writer of the letters."

"Certain. Heck asked around at a conference where there were a few of the Victoria folk. They all knew that Bradley had been writing poison pens. Some of those who'd received them had talked to each other and had suspected him. Then when he got the position up here, the Victoria letters stopped, which proved it beyond doubt. A really nasty bit of goods. I just hope this was really an accident and no poor chap is going to have to do time for getting rid of him."

"Thank you, Mr Jones. You've been very full and frank. Now, I do have to ask you where you were and what you were doing last Monday evening."

"By coincidence, round at Heck's place. We're planning a new course on the history of grammar for next year, and we were working on that."

"Just the two of you there?"

"Just the two of us."

"What time were you there?"

"I got there about seven, I suppose, and worked on until around ten, ten-thirty. Heck wanted me to stay on for a drink or two, but we'd had a fair bit by that time and I wanted to get on home."

"So you'd have arrived home, when?"

Crispin Jones stood up and crossed the room. He gently took the headphones from the girl's head. "What time would you say I got in last Monday, Poppet?"

She frowned at the interruption and held a hand out for the headphones which he lifted beyond her reach. "Last Monday?"

"The night I went round to Heck's, remember?"

"Middle of the movie," she said. "And you were pissed." He surrendered the headphones and she settled down again.

"Middle of the movie." Jones picked up a copy of the *Listener* from the top of the television set, the girl wriggling in annoyance as he momentarily blocked her view. "Here." He crossed back to the table. "Monday movie, TV 3. 9.45 to 11.30. So I'd've got back about 10.30, I suppose. Heck's place is just round in Ogilvie Street."

"Thank you." Rangi and Pike stood up. "What sort of car do you drive, Mr Jones?"

Jones snorted. "A very different car from the one I own," he said. "I *own* an MGBGT, but Merilyn's driving that. The car I drive is

136

Steph's – a bomb. Morris Marina."

"And the colour?" asked Rangi without much hope.

"Varied. That's it, parked outside." Jones looked through the window to verify his description. "Green door driver's side, bits of purple here and there on a tasteful base of what might once have been yellow."

"I see. Well, we'd better get on and see Mr Hancock."

Crispin Jones saw them to the door. As he opened it, he hesitated. "Look," he said, "old Heck's in a bit of a bad way. He's been... well, he's upset at the way Bronwyn threw him out, and he always was a bit of a drinker. Go easy with him? I can promise you the two of us were together that evening; it's not possible he could have done it. I suppose you'd prefer me not to call him to warn him you're on your way?"

Rangi would prefer that.

And Rangi was inclined to agree once he'd met Hector Hancock, that there was no way he could have managed to drive accurately enough to kill Bradley. He was a large man who seemed totally out of place in the poky little flat with the dingy carpet. Although his speech was not slurred and he walked with a steady dignity, the air around him was heavy with the smell of whisky – and it was still only mid-afternoon. Yes, he said, Crispin had been around last Monday. They had worked on planning a course for next year. His car? Well, it was a blue Honda Civic. Though these days he often walked to places or took taxis. Yes, he was aware that Joseph Bradley had written the letter that had wrecked his marriage. And, yes, he knew that the letters about him and Crispin were not the only ones written about university staff. He supposed he hated Bradley, but... who didn't? The man was hateful.

Rangi and Pike took a hasty leave, checking the carport to see that there was indeed a blue Honda Civic there.

"That's the lot for now then," Rangi said. "We can do the Real Estate agents tomorrow and check that the young guy's folk – the one who committed suicide – really were at that, what was its name? hotel."

"Excelsior."

"Yeah. You can do that while I'm at the bloody inquest." Rangi thought of the pile of papers waiting for him. Official papers. The things he *should* be doing. "How the hell I'm going to get time to see the Estate Agents tomorrow, God only knows."

"Sir won't be there, eh," Pike offered.

Rangi grinned. "That's right. He won't be. Not back till..." his grin vanished, "Wednesday."

"You reckon those two might've done it, Sarge? Jones and Hancock together?"

"When you have eliminated the impossible, Pike, the only thing remaining, however improbable, must be the truth."

He could tell Pike was impressed with that. "So you *do*...?"

"Early days yet, mate," said Rangi. "Anyway, you can drop me off at home for now."

"Nice and early, eh," said Pike.

"Why? You got a date tonight?"

"Got a new woman, Sarge, she's... wow!"

"Lucky man." Rangi let his mind drift. "So've I," he said softly, "so've I."

"You going out tonight too?"

"Not tonight, mate. Tonight I reckon I'll do a spot of housework." At least he now had three rubbish bins.

The inquest began at ten a.m. Detective Senior Sergeant Roberts gave his evidence, sat through droning testimony and heard without surprise that the coroner found that Joseph Bradley had died from massive injuries resulting from a hit and run accident. The whole thing took two hours.

Half-way through, Pike slipped onto the bench beside him. "The Excelsior say that Mr and Mrs Hale were there on Monday night," he whispered. "They checked in at 4.15 p.m. Mr Hale borrowed a courtesy car –"

"*Eh?*"

"Yeah, I got excited, too, Sarge. But he only did seventy kilometres, it was a silver-grey Nissan and he got back to the hotel at 9 p.m."

"Oh well. That's another off the list. Let's get some lunch when this is over and then see these estate agents."

They ate at Espresso Extra – the morning had been so boring that Rangi reckoned he deserved something a bit more cheerful than the Police cafe. He'd only just started to get himself round thick chicken soup with barley when he saw something a great deal more cheerful – and she was coming towards his table. Rangi had a quick look round; all the other tables behind him were full, she was definitely heading his way.

"Mind if I join you?" she said, putting her plate and cup down. *Join you* – very different from *Mind if I sit here?* Of course, with Julia filling his mind, Rangi wasn't going to be taking all that much notice of sleek blonde hair, grey eyes, black brows and lashes and a body that...

"Gudday," said Pike. "Sarge, this is Martha. I may have mentioned her last night."

Rangi stood up. "Good to meet you, Martha." The hand that took his was warm, the pressure firm. Pike was a lucky little sod. Still, look at Rangi, the luckiest sod of them all. This time tomorrow she'll be down here, his heart sang. Tomorrow night's a biggie again...

"So," he said, "how long have you two known each other?"

"Twenty-five days," said Pike.

Martha glanced at her watch. "And fourteen hours," she added.

Rangi laughed. "Sounds serious."

"No, not serious." She grinned. "I never get serious. Love 'em and leave 'em, that's my motto."

Pike didn't seem upset. "Same here," he said. "The dustbins of this town are littered with the women I've used and thrown away."

"So," Martha smiled into Rangi's eyes, "you can see we're in for a disastrous relationship."

"I reckon," said Rangi.

She started on her lunch. "So what's new in the world of crime?" she asked. "What've you been up to this morning?"

"Getting bored out of our minds," said Rangi. "Court work is about the worst thing we get lumbered with."

"Court work?"

"An inquest."

"That hit-and-run last week," Pike explained.

"Oh, that. Have you found who did it?"

"Not yet," said Pike.

Her eyes were on Rangi. "Do you think you will?"

He shrugged. "We'll find the car, probably. One day – one year. It'll have been dumped somewhere. When it turns up, we'll trace the owner, then we've found whoever did it. Unless it was stolen."

"You think it was stolen?" Martha had a way of staring at you, looking impressed.

Careful, Rangi told himself, this is Pike's girl; you don't want her transferring affections. "Probably not," he said, looking into her eyes. "If it was stolen it would have been reported by now. Hey, your lunch will be getting cold."

Her eyes dropped and she speared a piece of chicken. "And what did the inquest find?"

Pike snorted. "That he was killed in a hit and run accident."

"Surprise, surprise!"

"Waste of time," said Pike. "It took the whole morning."

"The whole morning to get it wrong," muttered Rangi and then wished he hadn't.

But Martha didn't seem to have noticed anything, she was smiling at Pike again. "Fancy a movie this evening?" she asked.

"Let's get a video and stay in."

The real estate agents were a dead loss. Rangi and Pike eventually got the manager away from the phone, introduced themselves, and showed him the copy of Bradley's letter.

"So that's why the IRD did their swoop. Who the hell wrote this?"

"Joseph Bradley."

"Never heard of him. What sort of busybody is he?"

"I believe he rented one of the flats on your books."

"Oh? Well, anyway, he was wasting his paper and our time." An impatient hand shook the copy of the letter. "We came out squeaky-clean, which isn't surprising; it's not worth your while to fiddle the tax books."

"You don't bear any personal grudge against Mr Bradley?"

"I think any guy who goes round stirring like this is a snake, but – not personal, no. Why should I?"

"Loss of income?"

"Not really – it was a bloody nuisance, but the investigation didn't stop business as usual. And the bosses understood."

"Bosses?"

"Barton and Banks are nationwide. I don't own the show, just manage this area."

And after that, Rangi had to go back to the piles of paper on his desk. Could Bradley have been killed by someone further back in his past? By some outraged Wellingtonian who had quietly nurtured his dreams of revenge until the time was ripe? How could Rangi persuade Sir to let him go down to Wellington and probe around when the inquest had so clearly stated that it was a hit and run? How could Rangi justify to Sir the time he'd already spent in questioning suspects of a crime that Sir would consider had not been committed? How could Rangi justify to Sir that the pile of papers on his desk was higher than when Sir had left?

Hey, tomorrow was the funeral! She'd be there! This time tomorrow – the funeral was in the morning, Rangi could take the afternoon off, Sir wasn't here to say no...

...He'd phone her tonight. Get into bed and cradle the phone...

Pike brought him a cup of coffee and Rangi sorted out some of the papers for him to deal with.

Ashley felt the usual glow at the way Sarge trusted him with important things – things that really should be done by someone much more senior than Ashley.

twelve

Rangi got to the crematorium far too early. He'd hoped that she might be there already, but she wasn't. In fact, he nearly got mixed up with the previous funeral whose mourners streamed out of the building a short while after he arrived. He found some of them coming up to him, shaking his hand and offering condolences. "So like your dear brother," one old guy murmured. "It will have hit you very hard, my poor Charlie, very hard indeed. But these things happen."

Rangi was bloody glad Pike wasn't there to grin at that. He blew his nose, excusing himself behind his handkerchief and went round the side of the crematorium to wait for Bradley's crowd.

Well, hardly a crowd. You wouldn't call five middle-aged men a crowd. Rangi guessed they were from the Uni; they all seemed to know each other. And no one seemed particularly upset; in fact, when the hearse drew up, they spared it only a glance and someone said something which sparked hastily shushed laughter.

The undertaker and his assistant slid the coffin out and onto its trolley which they wheeled inside. The five mourners chatted a little longer and then drifted into the crematorium. There was still no sign of her.

And then, just as Rangi was on the point of despair a white Honda slid over crunching gravel into the parking area. He raced towards it.

They couldn't kiss or anything, not there, but they stood looking at each other for a while. Her smile was slow and wonderful. "I think they're about to start," said Rangi. "We'd better get on in."

The five university people had filled a pew at the back, the undertaker was standing in the aisle beside them. He saw Julia and Rangi and tiptoed over. "My condolences," he whispered, handing each a booklet labelled *Order of Service*. "Friend or family?"

Julia looked confused, so Rangi said, "Ms Williams was Mr Bradley's literary agent."

"Ah." The undertaker did a sort of bow and led them to the front pew. They sat on the slippery wood and waited.

Julia had had a rush to get away on time and then there'd been some accident or other on the motorway so it was stop start driving for the first twenty kilometres. For the rest of the trip her mind had been dwelling on the time she'd be spending with Rangi or reliving the night they had had together. As she'd pulled up and seen him running towards the car she'd realised that she was really in no frame of mind for a funeral.

And now it suddenly struck her that this *was* a funeral – that in that gleaming brown box with its ridiculous handles and tasteful floral topping there was actually a body. A body that she had put there. She, the killer, was chief mourner at her victim's funeral. Her head went cold; she felt herself begin to shake. Old tales of murdered men bleeding afresh when their murderer came near... a macabre vision of blood seeping from the coffin, dripping down to splash on the fawn carpet...

"You all right?" His hand was warm on her trembling knee.

"Just feel a bit funny," she whispered.

He was looking at her in alarm. "You're pale as. Get your head down." She let his firm pressure on her shoulders push her down till her head was on her knees. He stroked her back and slowly warmth crept into her head and the shaking stopped.

As she sat up and smiled her thanks to him a door by the pulpit opened and a friendly little man in a surplice appeared. He took up his position in front of the coffin and nodded pleasantly. "Good morning," he said. "I wonder if, before we start, those of you at the back would like to move a little closer." He paused. "There are not very many of us here this morning, and I feel it might seem... warmer? more cosy? if I don't have to shout to reach the back of the building..."

There was a murmur and shuffling from behind. The clergyman nodded. "That's right," he said. "That's much better. No further? Oh well." He sent a special smile of sympathy to Julia and Rangi. "Man that is born of woman...," he read...

At the end of the service, as the other mourners waited politely for the clergyman to lead Julia and Rangi outside, Rangi was surprised to see Pike's Martha at the back. Jeez, she must have it bad, grabbing every chance to see lover boy. He waited for her outside while the clergyman spoke with hushed misunderstanding to an embarrassed Julia.

"Hi," Martha said.

"Gudday. You hoping to see – ah... Ashley?"

"Not really."

The hell she wasn't really! "He couldn't make it," said Rangi, and he felt himself smiling. "He's snowed under with paperwork this morning."

"Poor guy," she smiled back. "What are you doing here?"

"Eh?"

"I mean, it was a hit and run. I thought police only went to funerals when they were investigating a murder."

"Not necessarily."

"And you were in the front pew – was he a friend of yours?"

"Hell no! Well, I was a neighbour, but... No, I was there with –" Rangi nodded towards Julia who was still being comforted by the clergyman. "She's – she was – his agent."

Martha's eyes widened. "You think she killed him? It was murder?"

"God no! Well, if it was murder, *she* certainly didn't do it. She was busy knocking herself out against a lamp-post in Auckland at the time. Or a bit later. And her car's nothing like the car that did it."

"'If it was murder'. You think it might have been? But the inquest..."

Her large grey eyes were looking up at him in wonder. Out of the corner of his eye Rangi saw Julia shaking the clergyman's hand. "Well," he said, "there may be more to it than meets the coroner's eye."

"Murder?"

"Not impossible." Julia was moving towards them.

"You know the person that...?"

"Person or persons," said Rangi. "Hey," he added as Julia touched his arm, "this is highly confidential, mind. Shouldn't mention it, but, well – you know Ashley, you'll know about..." He reached two fingers to her lips and gently, jokingly, held them shut. Her eyes smiled at him and Julia's fingers tightened on his arm.

Rangi introduced the two of them and then Martha said she had to get back to work.

The rest of the day was every bit as wonderful as Rangi had planned. They were going to lunch in town, but there'd be the fuss of getting parking for two cars so Julia drove on to the flat while Rangi picked up some takeaways and they lunched in bed. They got up in time for pre-dinner drinks which Rangi, with a flash of inspiration, suggested they have in a little pub he knew half an hour's drive away with fantastic views of the sea. They stayed on for dinner and then went out to slide down dark sand-hills to the white lace of the sea glimmering in the moonlight. They'd probably have done it there, too, Rangi reckoned, but the tide was in and he didn't fancy a wet and sandy drive home. So they went back to the flat and, as Rangi said, made up for the time they'd lost having dinner.

And then grey morning dawned, spitting spiteful rain in thin pellets that streaked through the open window and pricked him awake. He rubbed his face on the pillow, propped on his elbow to slam the window shut and turned to her. As his arm went round her, he caught sight of his watch.

Shit and damn and hell. Of course he hadn't set the alarm last night. And now look. Twenty minutes to get up, get shaved, get to work...

On second thoughts, Sir wouldn't be back till mid-morning. He stroked her face till her eyes opened.

He was still in a warm dozy state when, an hour later she got into her car – they'd decided that Rangi would go up to Auckland on his next day off (Saturday or Sunday, he thought). He felt, as he watched her car back down the drive, like they were married already. It was a good, settled feeling; he didn't really mind her going now, because he knew they'd be together again soon.

He sang on his way to work, whistled as he put the car away and was smiling broadly as he made his way to his office. So what if Sir was on his way back, so what if Patrick Darlington-Jones's publishers were going to ring Sir? He'd be seeing her soon.

As he walked down the corridor, he became aware of something odd. People coming towards him either smiled somehow falsely or looked away as though they hadn't noticed him. Conversations in offices stopped as he passed the glass walls and started up again as he moved on. Christ, surely Sir wasn't back early and already panting for Rangi's blood?

But no, Sir's office door was open, the venetian blinds were still closed. No one there. Rangi slipped into his own office and Pike, who had been sitting on one of the "client" chairs, jumped to his feet, almost standing to attention.

"Morning," said Rangi. "How'd you get on with the paper?"

"Erk," said Pike.

"That paper-work I left you yesterday. How'd it go?"

"Oh that. That's done, Sarge. Here." Pike produced a pile of neat folders.

"Good man!" Well, that was something Sir wouldn't have to complain about when he got back. "Got enough on your plate for this morning?" He nodded a friendly dismissal.

"Um," said Pike.

"Yeah?" Rangi had opened the first folder, just checking.

"Do you get the morning paper, Sarge?"

"Yeah." Rangi grinned. "Didn't get time to read it this morning, but. Bloody alarm didn't go."

"Um. I got a copy here." A folded newspaper slid diffidently onto Rangi's desk.

"Eh?"

"Think you should read it, Sarge. Page three – local news."

The misery in Pike's voice jerked Rangi's head up. "Sit down," he said, smiling warmly. The kid was pale as. Rangi turned to page three.

Halfway down the page was a photo of Joseph Bradley. Rangi read the caption first. *Joseph Bradley: Accident or Deliberate Slaying?* Next to it the headline, POLICE QUESTION CORONER'S FINDINGS. Rangi sat down slowly. There was a by-line, *Staff reporter, Martha Fisk.*

"Your girl," said Rangi (no wonder the little sod was looking so sick), "what's her surname?"

Pike nodded. "Fisk," he said. "It's her wrote it, Sarge."

"A bloody reporter! You're trotting around with a bloody reporter and you tell her –"

But Pike was shaking his head. Rangi looked at the article.

Although the coroner found that Joseph Bradley, whose funeral was held today (Tuesday) died as the result of a hit and run accident, the Police are perhaps not so sure.

Mr Bradley was a University Lecturer in English, whom acquaintances describe as a man who kept to himself. He obviously did not have a large circle of friends, as his funeral was attended by only a handful. Among those present, though,

146

was Detective Senior Sergeant Rangi Roberts.

Senior Sergeant Roberts, interviewed after the ceremony said, "There may be more to it than meets the coroner's eye." He did not deny the possibility of murder.

"Shit," said Rangi, and his phone rang. A voice from a national newspaper asking for an interview about Joseph Bradley's death. "No comment," said Rangi, and he slammed the receiver down. "We'll just have to hope it dies down," he said. "And that Sir doesn't get to see it."

But Sir had seen it. He'd read it in the taxi from the airport that morning. Sir was not happy. If there had been anything to make Rangi feel that there was more to Bradley's death than came out at the inquest, he should have spoken about it either to Sir or, even at a pinch, to the coroner. But did he? No he fucking didn't, he chose to tell nobody apart from a bloody little doll of a reporter.

And what the hell was there, anyway, pointing to the bugger being murdered? What the hell was there? Poison pen letters, were there? Well why the hell hadn't Rangi told Sir about *them*? So what if Sir was out of town; there was a useful invention called the telephone, or perhaps Rangi hadn't caught up with that yet.

So which of the poison pen writers had done this murder? Well, it was obvious, wasn't it? Find out which one doesn't have an alibi for the time of the death, and there's your man – your person. Sir would have thought that even Rangi could have worked that out. So who didn't have an alibi? They all did? Well, goodness Sir! If they all had alibis, it didn't look very much like murder, did it?

And when did Rangi know they all had alibis? Monday afternoon. And when did he spill his guts to this reporter dolly? Tuesday. Goodness Sir again! He must really have wanted to impress her. Something special, was she? If Rangi couldn't get it without trading police secrets for it, he'd better get a job selling male cosmetics and get his bloody arse out of the force pdq.

After that Sir set in to give Rangi a real tongue-bashing. Rangi reckoned the only thing that saved him becoming a plod again – or being thrown out once and for all – was the pile of neat folders that he could put on Sir's desk to show him that he *hadn't* been spending all his time on wild goose chases after imaginary murderers. Then Sir's phone rang and it was that bloody publisher...

It was the worst morning of Rangi's life. In the end, Sir didn't

147

"suspend him pending further inquiries." "That'd mean you'd just mooch around on a fucking paid holiday. You're staying here, mate, and making yourself useful while I see what the lords and masters want done with you."

The Hales got out of the taxi, walked down the path, unlocked the door, and Bob carried the suitcases up to the bedroom while Bren put the kettle on. "There's no milk," she called. "Margie was going to get milk in once she knew when we were coming back. But we're back early. I should have rung her from the airport."

"You go over and get the mail," yelled Bob. "Ask Margie in for a cuppa – I'll go down to the store. I'll take the car, though. I'm in too much of a hurry for a cup of tea."

"Okay," called Bren. "I'll go over to Margie's now and get the mail."

Bren and Margie were already talking nineteen to the dozen when there was a loud knock on Margie's kitchen door and Bob burst into the room. "The car's gone!" he said. "The bloody car's gone!"

When he saw Margie's hand fly to her mouth, he realised that of course poor Margie would feel herself responsible. He opened his mouth to tell Margie that there was no way it was Margie's fault, but no voice came. Instead he left her to fuss over Bren, who'd gone all pale, while he went to phone the police. When he finished he told Bren to stay there and have a cuppa with Margie.

"Strong with lots of sugar, the way you're looking," Margie said.

"The police are coming round," said Bob. "I'll deal with them."

"You'd better tell them," said Margie, "that I think I might have seen the thieves."

"*What?*"

Margie nodded gravely several times and pressed her lips together. Then she said, "Yes. I didn't think anything of it at the time, but – do you know someone called Roberts?"

Bob thought for a moment. "Old Perce Roberts! Hell, is he still around? Friend my dad's, must be well into his nineties now."

"This was a younger man – in his thirties. Maori."

"Perce and Essie didn't have any kids." Bob thought again. "A Maori guy called Roberts?"

"With a younger man – a... European. They seemed to know you, we chatted for a while. It was in the weekend some time. They said they were sorry to have missed you...?"

148

Bob looked at Bren and then shrugged. "No one I know," he said.

Bren shook her head, and Margie nodded solemnly. "They must have been casing the place," she said. "I do feel awful. But I just didn't *think*..." She looked uncertainly at Bren as though torn between the two interesting roles of solacing her friend and giving important information to the police. "I did wonder a bit after they'd gone. I mean, it was sort of funny," she said, "them not wanting to leave any message. You know, looking back on it..."

Bob started towards the door. "Probably just collecting for something," he said. "But I'll tell the cops when they come, and they can come over and talk to you about it."

He touched Bren's forehead. "You all right?"

She nodded, trying to smile.

"It'll be all right," he said. "Don't you worry about a thing. Just have a nice cuppa and chat." Theft wasn't anything like as bad as Robby's death, but she was still vulnerable.

Rangi put the phone down. *Well, Watson, I think we've found our murder car.*

Murder car, Holmes?

Murder, Watson. Red Toyota. New red Toyota. Owner overseas and only now returned. Not only that, my dear Watson, but the owner is none other than Mr Robert Hale, father of the Robert Hale who committed suicide. Now, if it turns out that Jones and Hancock knew that Mr and Mrs Hale were off to the land of Oz, then we've solved it.

They were in it together, Holmes? Jones and Hancock?

Precisely, Watson. We have eliminated the impossible, after all.

Rangi stood up. He was no longer working in his office. Sir had relegated him to answering and sorting – and lengthened his hours. But Sir had done him a real favour. If he hadn't relegated Rangi to manning the phones, Rangi would never have heard of this. Parsons, the young constable who would normally have been dogsbody, would treat it simply as a stolen car and wouldn't know enough to put two and two together. He called to the kid now. "You take over here for half an hour or so, Parsons. I need to go out to see about a stolen car."

Parsons put down the file he was sorting and looked awkward. "Sir said..." He stopped.

"Sir's not here at the moment," said Rangi. "At the moment, and at least for now, I am the most senior person in the building. I'm going out to see about a stolen car. I have your permission, Your Highness?" Which wasn't fair, but stuff it.

Parsons slid into the vacated chair. "Sorry, Sarge."

Rangi punched his shoulder by way of apology. "I'll bring you back a chocolate fish," he said.

Mr Hale was a pleasant guy in late middle age. He took Rangi through the laundry to a door that led into the garage. "Haven't touched anything," he said. "Not once I opened the door and saw she'd gone. So if they've left fingerprints, they'll still be there."

"Good," said Rangi. "Probably wore gloves, but. Is there a light?" Mr Hale clicked a switch and Rangi crossed the concrete floor to look at fastening of the main garage door. "Doesn't look as though they forced it from this side. Was the internal door locked?"

"Oh yes, we always lock it if we're going away for any length of time. In case of..." Mr Hale grinned sheepishly and shrugged.

"Yeah. Any marks on the outside?"

"I didn't look."

"Better check, eh. The garage itself was locked?"

"Yes."

Rangi took one look at the scratches on the dark red paint of the garage door. "Yeah, she's been forced all right. Look at this."

Mr Hale bent over to peer at the marks. "Bastards," he said.

"Yeah. Neighbours see anything?"

"No," said Mr Hale. Then he added, "At least, I haven't asked around, but Mrs O'Brien next-door says she didn't. And she'd be the most likely one to notice. My wife's over there now having a cuppa."

Rangi started back towards the house. "Oh yeah. I met her."

"My wife?"

"No, Mrs O'Brien."

"Eh?" Mr Hale was opening the front door, standing aside for Rangi to go first. He stopped in his tracks.

"Yeah," said Rangi. "I actually called round here in the weekend to see you. She told me you were in Oz."

"To see me?" The guy tensed. "What about?"

"Oh, not about the car. Another thing." The knuckles on the door knob were white; lots of people reacted like that to the police asking questions. "Nothing that need concern you now." They continued into the house. "I'll jot down the particulars," said Rangi, "and then get someone round to check for prints."

They sat in the kitchen while Rangi filled in a case form. While he mechanically took down the details, his mind was working over how best to find out whether Jones and Hancock knew that the Toyota was going to be in an empty house. Not shock tactics this time, the poor guy had lost his son in a very distressing way and as there was no way *he* could have been the killer, Rangi didn't want to upset him more than necessary. He finished the report and handed it over for Mr Hale to sign.

"So, you've been over the ditch?" he asked.

"Yes. Yes, we had a short holiday in Sydney."

"Enjoy yourselves?"

"Oh, it was great, just great."

"And Mrs – ah – the lady next door kept an eye on, eh?"

"She and Bren are great friends. Bren's the wife."

"Didn't keep too good an eye on, but, did she?"

"You mean the car? Well, if they took it at night she wouldn't... and there's the hedge, too. That stops noise."

"Yeah. So she knew you were in Oz. Many of your friends know?"

"Everybody. Well, all our friends. Bren had a real big shopping list – things to bring back, you know."

"Might need a list of people who knew you wouldn't be here."

"Why?" Mr Hale's eyebrows rose as he realised the implication. "Oh no," he said. "No, none of the people we know would break in like that."

"Course not," said Rangi. "But they might have talked to someone who..."

"That's not very likely."

"Someone," said Rangi slowly, "knew that you weren't at home. Someone knew it was going to be safe to take the car. What about your neighbours across the way?"

"He's a retired bank manager, for God's sake. What'd he be doing nicking cars?"

"Hmm." Rangi looked thoughtful. "What about – say – people at the university, who worked with your son."

"What? What do you know about Robby?" He was looking angry now. Angry and something else – scared?

"I am a policeman, Mr Hale. We do know a lot of what goes on." There was a silence. "Would any member of the university staff know you were going away?"

"They're not likely to be car thieves."

"That's not what I mean. It's very easy for them to mention to someone – in a shop, getting petrol, just about anywhere – that you'd be away. Even talk about it to each other with someone overhearing. Thing is, to get a handle on this, I got to ask everyone who knew that you and your wife were going to Australia if they might have told someone. And if that someone could possibly have taken the car." It sounded good, Rangi thought. Mr Hale wouldn't know that police usually had little time to go into such detail over a car theft.

And it worked. Mr Hale obliged with a list of names of friends. A bloody long list; Rangi was glad he didn't really have to go round interviewing every one of them. And – he managed to keep his head down and keep writing – one of them was Crispin Jones. Mr Hale had bumped into him in town and had told him about their trip, in answer to Jones's concerned enquiries about Mrs Hale ("Bren took Robby's death very hard").

He had just finished writing and was tucking the list alongside the case report in a folder when the kitchen door opened. Mrs Next-door and another woman, presumably Mrs Hale, came in. "That's him!" shrieked Mrs Next-door. "That's the one who was asking for you! Oh, Bob, be careful; ring the police!"

Rangi took his leave while they were still calming her down. Bob never did remember to ask him what he'd called on Margie for over the weekend.

Parsons stood up as he came into the phone room. "Jeez, Sarge, I was due off an hour ago." Little bugger wouldn't have had the nerve to say that if Sir hadn't been so public in his strip-tearing.

"You can bugger off, then," said Rangi.

"Where is it?" Parsons was grinning.

"Where's what?"

"My chocolate fish."

"Piss off." But Rangi was grinning. If Jones knew, Hancock knew. They had only the alibis they'd given each other. Now somehow, somehow... Shock tactics?

He looked at the small pile of messages that had come in since he left for the Hale's. There, right on the top, the very last one. A farmer had reported finding a late model red car in a drainage ditch. This was it! It had to be!

Rangi rushed into the cloakroom and grabbed Parsons just as he was closing his locker. "Back," he said. "Back to work."

"Sarge?"

"Overtime. You've heard of overtime, mate. It's the thing that keeps this country's police force functioning. You've just picked up a bundle of it." He frog-marched the kid down the corridor and sat him back in front of the phones. "If Sir calls for me, I'm in the bog. My shift doesn't finish till ten. Martin's on after me; if I'm not back by then, you can leave when he arrives."

"*Ten*, Sarge?"

"Ten, mate." Rangi grabbed up the top message and headed for his office. "And this time I won't forget the chocolate fish."

From his office he called the farmer. Then he called a towing firm and arranged to meet them at the farm. He thought of calling Mr Hale and asking him to come along to identify the car, but decided against it. All the details – registration number, engine number and so on – were already on the case report in its folder. Besides, there was a chance it wasn't *that* car.

Fat chance. Rangi was certain. Inside him, Holmes curled his lips back, scenting success.

It was dark by the time the tow truck hauled the car out of the ditch. As it was dangling there, water spilling from its open windows, Rangi shone the torch to check the number plates. It was Hale's car, all right, and one side at the front had been badly dented. Rangi gave instructions to the tow truck driver to drop it off in the police yard, got in his car and set off back to the station.

"Sarge!" said Parsons. "I had a date tonight. This is the second time in a row I've had to stand her up. She's that mad!"

"Sorry, mate. But I need you to get out to the yard; there's a car coming in. Use gloves and get it wrapped and sealed in case some smart alec decides to tamper with it before the lab guys can get to it. Then you can take off. Here," he produced a cardboard box, "give her these from me and say I'm sorry."

Parsons took the box and looked inside. "Reckon it'll take more than chocolate fish," he said gloomily.

"Go on, off you go." Rangi helped himself to a few fish and levered Parsons cheerfully out of the chair. It was an hour before he could knock off, and there was nothing more he could do at the moment anyway. With Sir back in town, Rangi couldn't, single-handed, bring Jones and Hancock in for questioning tonight. The phone rang. "Good evening to you," Rangi purred as he bit into sweet rubbery marshmallow. "This is your friendly local cop shop. And how can I be of assistance?"

thirteen

He was at work bright and early the next morning, whistling down the corridor, tugging his forelock at Sir's still empty office. He was on phones again, so he helped himself to them and called first Jones, then Hancock. No reply from either, so he rang the uni and left messages for them to call him when they came in. Then he rang Mr Hale and told him his car had been found.

"Found?" Mr Hale was impressed. "You were quick off the mark!"

"Just luck, really. Coincidence."

"And when can I collect it?"

"Not for a while, I'm afraid, Sir. And you mightn't want it; it's not in good condition. You did say it was well insured?"

"Yes, but..."

"And we will need to run some tests on it."

"Tests?"

"We suspect that it may have been the car involved in an incident where a man was killed."

"...Good God! A hit and run?"

"A hit and run... or something much more serious."

"More serious?"

Rangi cursed himself for a big mouth. "Nothing definite, Sir. We just have to check things out very thoroughly, you understand."

"But... but what makes you think it was... you're saying it was *murder*?"

"Not at all, Mr Hale. There's nothing you need bother yourself about."

"Who was killed? Do you know who did –"

"Look, Sir, I spoke out of turn. There are two people that I'm going to ask to help us with our inquiries, but it's nothing that concerns you,

you were out of the country at the time."

"But..."

Of course, the guy would be wondering what he'd do for a car if his was locked up in prison. "No problem, Sir. I'm sure the Justice Department will pay for a rental if you need a car."

"But –"

The back of Rangi's neck prickled; he was not alone. He didn't need to turn round to know who had come in. "Must go, Mr Hale. Catch you later."

Sir was standing in the doorway. Rangi was being bloody free with the taxpayer's money, wasn't he? What the fuck was this about rental cars? And what was that bloody car doing gift-wrapped in the parking lot? Evidence of what? Was Rangi still on about that bloody hit and run being murder? Sir thought he'd made it clear yesterday that Rangi was no longer on the case. Sir thought that even Rangi would be able to understand words of one syllable. He – was – off – the – case. He – was – on – the – phones.

And what was this time sheet that Sir could see on the desk? Parsons claiming three hours' overtime! Would Rangi know anything about that? He'd had to *what*? He'd had to go out? He'd taken it on himself to give Parsons extra time so that he could go sniffing after a bit of skirt or something?

So that was the car responsible, was it? Great. That would be a start for whoever Sir decided to put in charge of the hit-and-run investigation. This time Sir would find someone sensible to take over – the cleaning lady perhaps. Anyone could do a better job of it than Rangi. The phone was ringing. Hadn't Rangi better answer it? It was what he was being paid to do... for the moment, for the next day or so until he joined the dole queue. Sir would just stand by for a little and make sure Rangi wasn't going to offer anyone free hotel accommodation at the Justice Department's expense.

It was a Crispin Jones on the line, said the switchboard. He had a message to call Senior Sergeant Roberts.

"No," said Rangi. "No, I can't take that call now."

"Give it here." Sir's hand enfolded the receiver like a Great Dane's jaw around a bone. "What is this call?... I see, well put him through."

Another phone rang. Rangi looked helplessly at Sir who glowered at him to take it, so instead of hearing what Sir was saying to Jones, Rangi had to listen to a Mr Archibald of 15A Broughton Road, whose washing had been stolen from the line for the third time this year, and

155

he knew who was doing it, too. He'd told the police both the previous times and nobody had even bothered to come round and it wasn't good enough. You pay taxes all those years and when – just once – you expect to get a fraction of them back in the shape of the police taking a serial laundry stealer seriously, you get shunted from pillar to post and nothing gets done.

Sir and Rangi finished their calls at the same moment. For a long time Sir just looked at Rangi as if his face was sprouting worms. Then he said, "So, I discover you've been trotting around the city in your own time interviewing respectable citizens as though you were acting with official sanction. Now you're asking them to call you up for friendly chats while they are at work and while you should bloody be working, too. You'd better come along to my office."

"But –" Rangi gestured to the phones.

Sir spun on his heel. "Pike!" he thundered. Pike, on his way down the corridor, stopped in mid-stride. "Get on the phones."

"Sir," said Pike. He looked helplessly at Rangi as he slid onto the chair.

"Any calls for this gentleman," said Sir, "get routed to my office. Understand?"

Pike nodded.

"Right." Rangi followed Sir down the corridor.

The call from Hector Hancock came in when Sir was still in full flood; it did not improve matters. Finally, the interview ended and Rangi went to his office to pack his gear.

He didn't know where to start. He'd had the office for over two years now, and things had just somehow piled up. He'd never planned on moving out. Well, maybe in a year or two, if he got some more promotion. Huh! He was shifting papers from one chair to another when there was a knock on the door. Mr Hale. Rangi could do without him just now.

"They told me where to find you," Mr Hale said. He was looking pretty sick.

Rangi dumped the papers from the chair onto his desk. "You better sit down. You look really crook."

"I am. I'm – I did it, you know."

"Did what?"

"The murder. I killed him."

The guy had flipped. "You were in Auckland that night. In that hotel – the Excelsior – we checked." He summoned his patience and said gently, "You didn't kill him, Mr Hale."

"I did."

The poor coot had probably discovered who'd been killed and that would have done it. If he'd known that Bradley had written the letter about his son, that would have done it. He'd have *wanted* to kill Bradley, and now that Bradley had been killed he'd probably got this guilt thing... couldn't think straight. "Listen," Rangi said, "if it was murder – and I only suspect it was – it wasn't you."

"Yes it was."

"If it was, I know who did it. This is confidential, understand. It's only because you're – you're in this state that I'm telling you, and you're going to have to forget that I ever said it –"

"You arrest anyone else, you're arresting the wrong person. I can't have that. I was over in Oz and found a shop that sold papers from all over. Well, naturally, I checked out the local one and there was the bastard's picture and you saying it might be murder. So I came back. I'm not sorry for what I did, but I'd be more than sorry if some other poor sod suffered for it."

Rangi sighed and leant back against his desk jostling a pile of papers that toppled and scattered onto the floor. The guy was going to have to be listened to, however crazy he was. Rangi eased his buttocks onto the cleared space. "Okay," he said. "Tell me about it."

It was a couple of nights after Bob had met Bradley when his tyre had been punctured outside the workshop that he'd decided to kill the bastard. Squash him flat like the thing he was. There didn't seem to be anything else to do.

But although it was easy enough deciding to do it; it was damn near impossible to work out *how* to do it. Night after night he'd tossed and planned and drifted into dream-filled sleep. Finally, he'd got it worked out.

He'd talked Bren into taking a holiday. High time, said their friends, after what you two have been through. They were going to go over to Oz – stay a couple of weeks in Sydney and have a good look round.

The night before their flight out, they booked into a hotel in Auckland. It was more expensive than anything they had ever stayed in before, but it was one that advertised courtesy cars.

Bob's doctor had given him sleeping pills after Robby's death – he still had some left. He felt bad doing it, but he slipped a couple into

Bren's coffee after dinner and quarter of an hour later she was off to bed and out like a light.

Once he'd seen her tucked up, Bob called at Reception. He'd had an urgent phone call from a friend – how much would a taxi to Albany cost?

God, that much!

But Reception was ready, willing, trained, to help. Mr Hale might not be aware that the hotel boasted, not one, but a fleet of courtesy cars. If he wished, he could use one of these and drive himself...?

Excellent. Mr Hale was delighted. He made a great fuss about asking what the time was. Just after seven? And how far away was Albany, how long would it take him to get there...? That meant that if he stayed half an hour, he could expect to get back at, let's see...

Finally, Reception off-loaded Mr Hale onto a porter who escorted him to the basement garage, helped him into a very nice little hatchback, told him just to park the car and drop the keys off at Reception on his return, and wished him a pleasant trip.

Bob noted the mileage before he started. The hotel might keep a record, though they would not be likely to check to see whether the seal of the odometer had been broken, so he'd alter it before he got back. He was longing to drive like the hammers, but there was the danger of being "snapped" by a speed camera, which would really stuff the alibi he had cooked up. He did good time, for all that, zapping the little car up to 130 when he could see that the road ahead was clear of authority.

He was back in his own street in just under an hour and a half. He cruised up it once, but there was no sign of life. Everyone inside cosy with Milo, bikkies and tele. He drove onto his front lawn, opened the garage, backed his own Toyota out, put the hotel car inside and shut the door. The whole operation was done without lights.

He drove round the corner, parked and forced himself to wait for ten minutes. It was nerve-wracking, but he had worked it out. This was the time that the cops would appear if any of the neighbours *had* seen anything and reported it. And if the cops did come round, he hadn't done anything. No law against acting like an idiot backing cars in and out of your own garage the night before taking the wife on vacation. It might be odd, but it wasn't criminal.

He checked his watch. Twenty to nine, and he'd parked at half-past on the dot. Time to be moving. He didn't let himself think about what he was moving to – just one step at a time. Now it was time to drive round to the maggot's flat. Then it would be time to get out and knock at the maggot's door. Then – it wasn't time to think of that yet.

He was in the maggot's street. Every bit as deserted as his own had been. He coasted slowly up to the maggot's driveway.

And suddenly there was a sign of life. The maggot's big Jag rolled down the drive. Christ, he nearly swiped Bob as he backed into the street.

Well, that was that then. All the planning down the tubes.

...Bugger it, it didn't have to be. The plan had been to knock him out – Bob was twice the maggot's size and bloody fit for his age – get him into the car, drive him out to some country road and run over him. The cops would treat it like a hit and run. They'd look for the car responsible, but it would be safely in one of the drainage ditches on the peat farm land two blocks away from the Hale's house. No one would even know what car had done it until the Hales got back from their holiday in Oz and reported the red Toyota stolen from their garage.

That *had* been the plan, but now – it wasn't necessarily too late. Maybe the maggot would get out of his car at a place where Bob had a chance to clobber him. Bob pulled out to follow the slow-moving Jag. It was taking a risk – God alone knew where the maggot was heading, could be to some crowded place where there wouldn't be a hope in hell...

Bob realised that he was going to do it, no matter what. If they caught him, they caught him – too bloody bad; the ache in his gut at the loss of Robby was so strong that it demanded action. If he got done for it, Bren would understand.

They were approaching Poet's Corner. Not the sort of district the maggot would normally hang round in. Bob was keeping about half a block distance between them and when he saw the Jag turn left into McGonigall, he pulled up. He'd been here a couple of times before with the tow truck and remembered that McGonigall was a dead end both ways – with parking behind the turning circle at the left end, a few houses away. He switched his lights off, edged his car up to the corner so he could see what the maggot was up to.

He was walking *up the road towards Bob*, that was what he was doing! Christ, and there was no one around. It was almost as if he was offering himself for the hit and run. Act now, man – it's *meant*.

Bob's foot came hard down on the accelerator, the Toyota leapt forward beginning its left turn in a slew of gravel and a whine of rubber. Then, Christ! Something – some bugger without lights – came out of nowhere on his right and slammed into Bob's door. There was a crump of metal, shower of glass. Fuck it. Ignore it. Bob glanced ahead – the bugger had stopped, staring at the two cars. The crash hadn't stopped the engine, Bob gunned it again and drove straight at the maggot. The heavy slam of the body was the most satisfactory noise Bob had heard in his life.

He didn't get out to see if he'd done it – he just backed the car over the body.

As he sped round the corner, he briefly wondered if the guy in the other car had seen him. But he got the impression, under the street lamp, that there was a body slumped over the steering wheel. Bob hoped he was okay. But it was only a side-swipe. In any case he'd be mad to stop and find out now.

On the way to the peat land, he was filled with a feeling of being invincible. The night air was cold through the broken window, but he didn't give a damn. He found himself singing, "Will you still need me, will you still feed me...?" and laughed out loud.

He bumped across a cattle stop into the paddock he'd chosen, not even bothering to see if there was anyone round to notice him. He drove up to the ditch – more like a narrow canal – and parked parallel to the line of the cut with the driver's side wheels right on the edge, then took the keys, opened all windows, got out, collected the jack and bricks from the boot and jacked the car up as far as she'd go on the passenger side. With the car off balance like that it took no effort at all to topple her over and into the water. She bubbled a bit and then settled down, well under the surface. Bob tossed the jack and bricks after her and set off back home – a late evening jogger in a bit of a hurry.

He checked the street carefully before opening the garage door. No one. He unlocked the door and then thought for a moment. If it was going to look as though the car was stolen, how would the cops reckon the thieves had got in? Good job he'd thought of that. He went into the garage, rummaged in his tool box, shut and locked the garage door again and then tried to force the lock with the blade of his heaviest screwdriver. The lock gave almost straight away. Hell, he'd make damn certain he got a better one when this was over. He scratched at the paint a bit with the screwdriver to make sure the thing looked forced.

Then he checked the street again, backed the courtesy car out, closed the door and drove as fast as he dared to Auckland, stopping once to buy a carefully calculated amount of petrol. Just before he reached the hotel, he stopped again, fiddled the mileage so that it would seem he'd travelled only to Albany. Nobody saw him as he parked the car and took the lift from the basement. It was eleven p.m.

At ten past eleven, Mr Hale from room 367, in pyjamas and dressing gown came sleepily down to Reception. He'd woken up and suddenly remembered that he hadn't returned the keys of the courtesy car he'd borrowed.

The receptionist smiled understandingly and told him he needn't have come all the way down. She checked the car off the list, putting 9 p.m. in the *Time Returned* column, as that had been the time Mr Hale had actually got back.

Bob didn't tell the cop all this, not all the planning and agony that led to it. A cop didn't need to know it all, just the important facts. "I drove down from the hotel in their courtesy car," he said. "I altered the odometer. I tricked the receptionist into thinking I got back a bit after nine. Bren doesn't know anything about it. I put the hotel car in the garage and used my own. I went round to his place and saw him drive out. I followed him, and I – I did it. You mustn't arrest anyone else."

Rangi believed him. The guy was white, shaking, but his voice was firm. Rangi pushed the last pile of papers onto the floor and sat down behind his desk. "We'd better go over this again slowly," he said. "Give me time to write it down. What time did you and your wife arrive in Auckland?..."

fourteen

Julia found it a terrifying weekend. He'd rung to say that he'd got both days off, not just Saturday, and how about painting the town red?

He arrived just before lunch, twice as gleaming and glowing as she remembered him. He swept her into the bedroom, and they skipped lunch entirely.

And then, as he lay on his back, one arm under his head, the other cradling her, he said casually. "Well, reckon I'm in for some promotion pretty soon."

"That's nice."

"Too bloody right it's nice. Promotion doesn't come too easily round our joint, but Sir owes me. Oh yes, Sir owes me."

"That's nice." She nuzzled into his armpit. He smelt delicious.

"Aren't you going to ask me why I'm the golden-haired boy?"

"Why are you the golden-haired boy?"

"Because Joseph Bradley's death wasn't an accident, and because I found out who killed him."

"Not an accident?"

"Murder. I always knew it was murder, you see."

Her mouth filled with bile. He'd been playing with her, toying with her. He knew all the time... The bed was lurching, the walls spinning round. She buried her face in the pillow, closed her eyes. The world behind her eyelids still spun. Christ, what now? What happened now? She swallowed frantically.

She muffled her voice in the pillow so he wouldn't hear the panic. "What happens now?"

"Now?" A finger lazily outlined her ear. "Now there's an arrest. There's a trial. There's a prison sentence. What else? You going to sleep?"

Sleep? God, she'd never sleep again.

He yawned. "Might be nice to zizz a bit. Go out for dinner later?"

She had found his power sexy. She had thought she had. Now, this was the real thing. Real naked power teasing her, trifling with her – with her *future*, for Christ's sake. He must know how she'd be feeling now he'd told her, and he didn't give a stuff. He was getting his kicks from her helplessness, her utter misery. God, the man was sick! He'd taken her knowing that, at the end of it all, he'd be arresting her. Knowing what she'd done, he'd still fondled, pretended love, he'd... She was going to throw up. "Got to go to the bathroom," she muttered, pushing herself away.

"Kiss me first," he ordered.

"No," she said. She couldn't, she'd puke all over him; it would be utterly degrading. Hell, the whole *scene* was utterly degrading. She felt dirty, worse than dirty.

She rushed to the other loo, the one by the back door where he wouldn't be able to hear her retching, wouldn't be able to lie there with that lazy grin, enjoying what he had made of her. She got there in time, and with the voiding came a clarity of self-knowledge. It was the idea of power that had turned her on, not the reality. She thought with nostalgia of Freddie in his drunken weakness weeping in her arms.

She went back to the bathroom, showered, cleaned her teeth, her eyes avoiding the mirrors. She was drying her hair when the door opened. "What you doing?" His smile seemed tender, but when you knew what lay behind it, it was the scariest thing in the world.

"I felt like a shower." Her voice was steadier now. Busy with the towel, she didn't have to look at him.

"Good idea." He patted her bottom possessively as he passed her to turn on the water. Then his hand encircled her wrist. "You can soap my back," he said and he pulled her under the shower.

His skin was glossy with streaming water. His arms went round her, urgent again. She didn't dare pull away. She tried to distract him, reached for the soap, pretended to lather his chest, but her hands were held in a strong grasp. The soap slithered up and plopped onto the floor. She stooped for it.

"Don't you know about the dangers of picking up the soap in showers?" he joked and she found herself bent over, his thighs thrusting, his hands clutching her breasts. She was a thing, an animal. It was all her erotic daydreams come true and it was vile. She hated herself, hated him.

Somehow they were dried and dressed. Somehow they were sitting in the sun on her deck and drinking wine. Somehow she found the strength to ask it. "When will the arrest be?"

"The arrest?"

God, how he revelled in his power. Making her spell it out. "The arrest for Joseph Bradley's..."

"Oh, that." He grinned and lifted his glass. "Had my mind on other things. That was yesterday."

"*Yesterday*?" She was shaking again.

"Yeah. Got a confession and all. This is confidential, mind." And he added, as though to entertain her with a light piece of police goss, "It's a funny thing, but after a murder we often get kooks in confessing to it. The more gruesome the killing, the more ning-nongs we get. This time there was only the one."

"And you *believe* it?"

His eyes were hooded against the sun. "I'd be a mug not to, wouldn't I?"

He had accepted a confession from some poor psychotic to... to *shield* her? No, not shield. Not this brilliant amoral animal. He'd had no scruples, no compunction about allowing some fool to ruin his life so that Rangi could claim Julia's gratitude, bind her to him with ties that were... were filthy.

Or was this his way of getting *her* to confess? Was the whole thing a lie? Did he expect her to burst out, *But you can't condemn an innocent man; I did it*?

That was more like it. He was diabolically clever, look at him watching now through lowered lids, prying, probing her reactions. Hell, she would never be safe. She'd never get him out of her life, he'd be there ready to spring, an ever-present danger... One thing, though; he surely couldn't have the sort of proof of her guilt that would stand up in court. If he did, she'd be behind bars already.

She could go. She could pack up and go. She'd go to Freddie; her clients wouldn't mind where she lived. She could work just as well from Australia as from New Zealand. She could go this week. Just get through the weekend, put the sale of everything into an agent's hands. She *could* get away, and Rangi need never know where she'd gone. If she planned it carefully – and one thing she knew she was good at was careful planning...

But for now, for this weekend, she'd have to play along. Not let Rangi see she knew he was suspicious of her. She'd fall in with all his plans, all his wishes. If he brought up the subject of Bradley again, play it cool, pretend she really wasn't interested. Just another twenty-four hours; surely she could manage that.

Rangi had never had such an amazing weekend. The only thing that marred it was that Julia was somehow... *too* obliging. He realised with a sinking feeling as she brought him a luxurious breakfast in bed on Sunday morning that she was doing what many others had tried before – making herself indispensable; softening him up for marriage, or at least a permanent relationship.

So why should that bother him? Hadn't he been thinking about settling down – and with her? He bit into his third croissant. But would it really work out? Look at her books, for example – shelves and shelves of the bloody things, and she'd read them *all*. The main thing, though, was her submissiveness, which he hadn't really noticed before. *You master, me slave.* It got to a guy in the finish – sort of sickly, somehow. Nice enough – bloody nice, to be honest – for a short time, but... And then there was the way that every now and then she seemed to get all trembly. Not at the sort of moments you'd like a woman to go all trembly, but just – out of the blue. He wondered if maybe she was quite... *normal.*

Still, when he kissed her goodbye Sunday afternoon he promised they'd be together again soon. "Bit busy for a while with the Bradley murder, of course," he said. There she went – all shaky again.

Frederick Tapper finished copying the last sentence of *The Pungent Collection*, sighed, and flexed his fingers. It had been the worst fortnight of his life. The drudgery of the work, the resentment he felt at every skilful word, had drained him. If only he could hire a typist to do it for him. But typists have to be reasonably intelligent, and even a dumb one would wonder at the necessity of copying a perfectly good manuscript. Still, it was done; he wouldn't have to copy another for months.

The phone rang. It was Julia. So she wanted to come over, did she? Well, tough. He had the manuscripts, she'd destroyed the disks; if she ever said anything about anything, she'd be up for murder.

"Dearest," said Frederick, "you know what I said. We must just be patient. I don't think it would be – *politic* for us to seem to be an item just yet."

There was a pause. "Freddie," Julia's voice was soft but somehow charged with power, "I lied to you."

"Lied to me?"

"I didn't destroy the disks. I still have them. I have copies as well."

She flew out two days later. They were married shortly afterwards. They went to the States to see Frederick's publishers on their honeymoon so that they were well away from any newspaper reports of a very minor manslaughter trial in New Zealand.

Robert Hale's lawyer had quickly managed to change the charge from murder, pleading that Hale, having started out to Albany, had suddenly had a fugue brought on by the stress of his son's suicide and of going overseas for the first time in his life. He had realised that he was driving the wrong car, headed off home, got his own car out, and was rushing back to Auckland to collect his wife when he hit Bradley. The shock of the impact had brought him to his senses and so he'd taken what measures he could to protect himself (such as dumping his car and altering the odometer).

There was a great deal of sympathy for Hale, who was given a suspended sentence. However, he never felt easy in the small city again. Fairly soon he and Bren sold up the garage and moved to another district.

Rangi was surprised that there was never any reply when he rang Julia. Surprised and, he admitted to himself, rather relieved. She was a bit unbalanced, he reckoned. Really, that was the only explanation for the way she'd gone on that last weekend – Probably anyone who had to be around writers so much would finish up a bit odd.